The Commission

The Commission

A Hip Hop Interpretation of The Mafia

By
O'SHUN M JONES

Copyright © 2012 by O'Shun M Jones.

Library of Congress Control Number: 2011904774
ISBN: Hardcover   978-1-4568-7784-2
              Softcover   978-1-4568-7783-5
              Ebook   978-1-4568-7785-9

All rights reserved. No part of this book may be reproduced or transmitted in any form or by any means, electronic or mechanical, including photocopying, recording, or by any information storage and retrieval system, without permission in writing from the copyright owner.

This is a work of fiction. Names, characters, places and incidents either are the product of the author's imagination or are used fictitiously, and any resemblance to any actual persons, living or dead, events, or locales is entirely coincidental.

This book was printed in the United States of America.

To order additional copies of this book, contact:
Xlibris Corporation
1-888-795-4274
www.Xlibris.com
Orders@Xlibris.com
95107

Contents

Chapter 1	Coming Up	1
Chapter 2	A Rude Awakening	5
Chapter 3	Cold Nights and Empty Skies	11
Chapter 4	A Reality Check . . .	15
Chapter 5	Collecting Your Bones	18
Chapter 6	All Grown Up Now	23
Chapter 7	My Gut Instinct	26
Chapter 8	Rags To Riches	30
Chapter 9	Tears and Departures	33
Chapter 10	A Vision And A Mission	37
Chapter 11	Setting A Mark	40
Chapter 12	Keys To The City	43
Chapter 13	Keep A Strong Arm	48
Chapter 14	All For the Taking	56
Chapter 15	The Commission	61
Chapter 16	Respect It or Check It	64
Chapter 17	Unfinished Business	70
Chapter 18	Loyalty Before Royalty	76
Chapter 19	Blowin' Money Fast	80
Chapter 20	Made My bed	86
Chapter 21	Blind Sides In Life . . .	95

Chapter 22	Thug Passion	100
Chapter 23	Taking The Backseat	105
Chapter 24	Catching Up On Old Times	111
Chapter 25	Keep Your Head On The Swivel	116
Chapter 26	Conflict Of Interest	120
Chapter 27	Lights, Camera Action	124
Chapter 28	The Sky Is falling	132
Chapter 29	Blood Thicker Than Water	136
Chapter 30	Teflon Don	141
Chapter 31	When The Smoke Clears	145
Chapter 32	Heavy Is The Head That Wears The Crown	149
Chapter 33	Judgment Day	158
Chapter 34	The Aftermath	165

Prologue

Man Make the Money . . . Money Don't Make the Man

". . . They got the nerve to ask me why I do the things I do. I got the nerve to serve you up like a waiter do . . ."   Andre 3000—Ain't No Thang

". . . Never disrespect a mans' property . . ."
Forest Whitaker—Jason Lyric (Film)

Ronnie

"*HE'S GOING TO blow that mothafucker head clean off his goddamn shoulders,*" I said out loud as I watched my younger cousin McLaren Roadster pull into the half-empty parking lot. I could read straight through Donell's facial expression, and I knew that with a temper like his, he was planning to do just that.

"Look man," Donell said in his thick, country accent.

"I hear what you're saying, but this snake ass nigga lied to me, to my face and now it's personal." Catching a glimpse of Donell's Smith—Wesson 357 magnum, his six foot six muscular frame towered over Slim, who was attempting to get inside his SUV.

After disappearing for three weeks with the hundred grand he owed Donell, Slim finally had the nerve to come back home into the city bragging how he was back on his feet now.

Listening to *Murder Was the Case* by Snoop Dogg. I just shook my head as we sat there in the Good Luck fast food parking lot.

"Cap...Why didn't you bring a silencer? With all the heat the Mob is catching these days, that there is the last thing we should be using." I said with my eyes trained on the gun that rested in his lap.

"So this how you want to play the game huh . . . I got to have *my goons* hunt yo ass down?"

"Awwe naw big homie, it ain't even like that. A family emergency came up, and I had to leave town."

Cautiously while keeping his eyes trained on Donell, Slim opened up the door to his Range Rover as he placed his food on top of the SUV.

"Tell that shit to somebody who gives a fuck. Mothafucka I'll blow yo stupid ass brains out!"

Through clenched teeth Donell grabbed Slim shirt collar hurriedly forcing his back into the dirty brick wall before slightly lifting him off his feet-snatching the diamond necklace off of him in the process.

"Nigga if you think all this money has made me soft, I'll show yo bitch ass that it ain't!" Donell said throwing Slim sideways toward the ground. Seeing that Slim quickly caught his balance, not falling—Donell then lunged forward, grabbing Slim by the neck slapping him against his temple two times with the butt off his pistol using his free hand.

"The bigger the Mob gets, the bigger this dude ego gets."

Donell was taking the principle of this whole situation too far because he was taking it personal. But one thing I remember Barry telling me was that in this game, it's all business.

"Damn D . . . You ain't got to take it there." Slim said with a petrified look of fear written over his face as he slowly rose to his feet one knee at a time.

Watching Slim regain his composure, Donell withdrew one .357 from his holster and another from behind his back.

"Nigga you think you can rob me and live to see the next day . . . ? But that day ain't today."

Donell said aiming the barrels in Slim direction seeing that he now was onto his feet, running away.

POW POW!

The powerful calico bullets sounded off piecing through Slim's body, causing him to stop in mid-stride, turn and fall back against the fence outlining the parking lot.

With sweat running down his face in pain, Slim naturally grabbed his thigh, then his right shoulder. With a deranged look written over his face, Donell fired rounds into Slim's body as if they weren't cars passing by behind them.

"Money has changed him Cap, and not for the better you feel me." I said as we both sat there surprised that Donell could go from being a flashy ladies man to a killer within the blink of an eye.

Chapter 1

Coming Up

"..Damn right I like the life I live, cause I went from negative to positive..."
               Notorious B.I.G- Juicy

Barry

"NAW FUCK THAT! Ain't nobody going to fight anybody up in here! You feel me?" Barry said standing in-between Derrick and Kool K in the hallway outside the locker room. At Madison High School, it was more than just tension- but resentment due to the cluster of students from different neighborhoods near and far from the actual school district.

Kool K was from a neighborhood composed of Crips who called theselves the Four Deuce Crips. Derrick on the other hand was from Turner Court projects and everybody knew what he was about, gangbanging. He was with a doubt a Blood and known to shoot people.

"Now I don't care who said what, we're going to have practice and when practice is over with, won't nobody be waiting to get back at anybody," Barry said looking to both of the young men as they stood on opposite sides facing one another with their crews ready to throw down. Barry was the only dude that could settle beefs that he wasn't involved in himself. He was the only person that knew so many people if not through his cousin Ronnie, to be able to talk sense into other people. Whether he had helped someone in another instance or he was a close friend of the people he was dealing with, dudes that knew little of him would listen to Barry because he was always serious, and his word was his bond.

"Alright Barry, that chump gets a pass this time." Derrick said as he composed himself while looking from Kool K then to Barry "It's only because you're my homie that me and my crew will roll out of here instead of rolling on that sucker." Derrick said as he simulated shooting a gun with his fingers at Kool K.

Barry knew that Kool K was a Crip indeed but he wasn't a killer.

Derrick, on the other hand, was expelled from Lincoln High School, and he often ran with Ronnie. It was without a doubt to anyone what Barry cousin Ronnie was about.

As Derrick's crew exited out the hallway, Kool K crew left out the opposite direction as Kool K himself followed Barry and the rest of the varsity team players into the locker room for practice.

The only junior at James Madison High School who was starting as a varsity running back and next in line to be the team captain was Barry McCoy. Barry got along with the classmates that were older than him and was respected by those his age because of how he treated everyone.

Although Barry spoke very little if any, street hustlers and players from what seemed like every neighborhood naturally took a liking to Barry. Half the people he knew were by way of his cousin Ronnie and the other half he knew already because he had gotten them out of trouble at one time or another.

His peers looked to him as a negotiator to settle disputes so they would die down or just blow over. The student body president even created and gave Barry the title of class mediator, for students in detention and in-school suspension.

Donell, Barry's younger brother, was not quite the same emerging image of his brother let alone his cousin Ronnie. Donell on the other hand, was more charming in the aspect of dealing with women. When it came to his female counterparts, Donell had more than his share. Although he was exceptionally talented when it came to playing basketball, he was serious only when the time required him to be. Voted best dressed in his class, he had established his reputation to be an eye-catching and smooth gentleman of leisure early. Although he wasn't as serious as his brother Barry, Donell dealt less with people in the same circle as Barry and more with people involved in the party scene along with his best friend Stanley.

"Come on now son, you got to think faster." Dave said urging his son on to continue thinking ahead in the intense chess game between the two.

"These are the type of situations you have to be ready for."

"You may not see it clearly yet, but life is all about thinking ahead- faster than the next man. You're a natural born leader in the pack, and with that being said, the only thing more important than the decisions you make are the timing that you choose to make them in . . . . Life is just like this game."

"I hear what you're saying, but I'm out numbered, with no defense."

Barry said looking at his black chess figures slightly agitated at how he let his bishops, queen and pawns get taken away so quickly.

"See about fifteen minutes ago, you were hitting that clock at the drop of a dime thinking it was about getting somewhere fast- but it's not. It's about winning, getting to the finish line when the timing is right, no matter what the obstacles are."

"Ohh shit! Study long, study wrong bro," Donell shouted from across the basketball court observing his older brother play their dad.

As Dave used his King and Queen to control the center, Barry was forced to slowly move further back on the board to stay in the game. Dave on the other hand, knew all along he would check mate Barry; he just wanted to watch to see if Barry would give up when he was losing.

TIC TIC TIC . . . . Dave used his Queen to checkmate Barry King as that was his final move that brought the game to an end.

"Damn bro, you're getting better. I remember when you couldn't even last five minutes against pops in chess."

As Ronnie and Stanley walked over to the table closer where Barry sat frustrated and alone, Ronnie's eyes met Barry's before he spoke to him-

"Bro you can't beat yourself up, I mean you're good for your age, but Dave is like an unofficial Grandmaster cuz."

Even though Ronnie's statement was meant to be uplifting in terms of a teenager playing against someone twice his age, Barry just shook his head still deep in thought in his own world.

"Forget being the best against everyone my age, I want to be the best period."

Pop's disability check from the V.A., along with his truck driving earnings and mom's measly check from nursing, income was just enough to stay in what was in my eyes middle class. Our dad was once temporally paralyzed from being shot in his back due to friendly fire while serving in Korea. While in the process, when they discharged him, and he arrived back in the states, he had a full recovery.

I figured our dad made his money from truck driving, although I couldn't figure out why our dad would run errands in the middle of the night. Dad often would work *on call jobs* the majority of the time. I always believed that it was because of these extra odd jobs that really helped us stay ahead. Mom would get upset at him sometimes, but Donnie and I wouldn't understand why—I mean it was his job.

As time quickly passed by, the evening skies grew pitch black while

Donell and I showered and got ready for the night's dinner. I could smell the Crisco cooking grease frying Mom's homemade recipe fried chicken when the fumes and flavored filled aroma lit the kitchen, living room and hallways. Mom turned over and whipped the garlic-mashed potatoes until they were smooth and firm before lightly sprinkling pepper over the top. She then turned the crock-pot down to low, allowing the collard greens to simmer so it would be ready when we came to eat.

When I would take the time to think about it, our mom was more of a contempt and conservative woman. She loved just being a mother and a wife. She would cook meals early in the mornings and always make sure my brother and I would have a meal prepared when we came home. She even would make a plate and set them aside for our dad no matter how late he would come home- not to mention one for our cousin Ronnie who didn't stay with us.

As I went ahead of Donell to begin eating, I was overjoyed about going out tonight with all the seniors we went to high school with. Ronnie was headed over to get my brother and me to go see the new movie Menace II Society. He had the hook up and knew someone at the ticket booth in which we could get tickets to rated R movies without showing our ID's.

And just like clockwork, as my brother and I slapped boxed in the front lawn, Ronnie rolled down the street in his 1985 Chevrolet two-door Caprice turning down our street making wide turns. I couldn't help but smile at him as he had his windows rolled halfway down blasting Eazy-E *Nobody Move.*

Chapter 2

A Rude Awakening

"Man sometimes you got to fight for what's yours . . . You know how that shit goes . . ."
Simon—Blue Hill Avenue

Barry

I REMEMBER WHEN I went to Mr. Blues record shop on Martin Luther King Street, and the owner Mr. James wouldn't sell me a copy of the Mystikal cassette tape "Unpredictable". That was a day I'd never forget.

"It has way too much cursing in it and even though you're a junior or senior in high school, that album will have too much poison going throughout your ears," Mr. James said all the while sitting comfortably behind the counter with his arms folded.

I was pissed off, to say the least, because I had my own allowance money, and my brother did too.

"I know ya'll daddy. He's a man that goes by rules, and you got to be breaking one by coming up in here asking for that album. I ought to tell him how you're standing there eyeballing me like you've never been taught to respect your elders."

"Are you even sure you want that album? What do you know about what he raps? How are you going to relate? If I was ya'll daddy I wouldn't let you listen to it."

As I turned from Donell back around to face Mr. James, he began talking fast as if he was trying to defend his reasoning. "Hell, your hoodlum cousin Ronnie already run around this city acting like he's C-Murder."

Many people were afraid to say what they thought about Ronnie to his face because of his reputation for violence, but he would always tell me and Donell that we were more like the brothers he wished he had and for that he always had our back, right or wrong.

"Alright, whatever man."

When I would think of how my dad kept a tight hold of me and my brother as far as our coming and goings went, I felt as though he did so because we were his kids and his responsibility, while Ronnie wasn't.

Donnie was an instigator as well as a ladies' man. He was light skinned with curly hair and stood taller than I at six feet and two inches. He was one of the best at playing basketball the city had ever seen.

Coming home, I couldn't help but notice our neighbors houses compared to ours. Our dad always had my brother and I doing things to our house on the weekends like painting the house and planting flowers in the front yard.

Standing in the driveway, I seen our Dad's friend Mr. Melvin leaning up against the side of his truck listening to Rick James' *Ghetto Life,* while at the same time talking to our dad as he cleaned his car tires.

"Yo pops what's up?"

"Hey Donnie son, what's happening?"

The more my mom told me, the more I began to see it for myself that just like my dad was always serious, so was I. And just like I didn't joke around much, our dad's no nonsense demeanor showed in his attitude.

When I thought about it, my dad didn't say he loved us much, but at the same time he didn't have to say it that much in my book because he showed us during the valuable time we spent together. That's how I knew he loved us.

"Boy what's the matter, someone bothering you and you're debating on getting back at them?"

"Naw daddy, haven't no one punked me, it's just that Mr. James was trying to play me and Donnie at the record store today, saying how we couldn't buy a C-Murder cassette tape because *he knew you* and if he was our dad . . ."

"Wa wa wait a fucking minute,"

"Did you just tell me he said *if he was* yo daddy?"

"Ye yeah that's what he said." I caught myself stuttering because dad hated to hear us stutter.

Dad detested people that stuttered soo much that he would tell my brother and I that a man who stutters is lying or has something to hide. He would even go as far as to say that a man born with a speech impediment was born a coward ass liar and we shouldn't trust him.

"Now why in the hell are you stuttering?"

"I don't know."

"Mothafucka don't know me," Dad said in a deep raspy tone.

"Donnie go behind the T.V. in the living room and get my magnum."

"And you... Get the hell in the front seat."

Once Donell began walking down the steps with Dad's gun in his hand, our neighbor Mr. Fred looked on while grinning from ear to ear at the sight he was seeing.

"You're using your son's as your muscle men know Big Dave?"

With his back to Mr. Fred, pops stood halfway in his car about to shut it when he froze as if he was playing *Simon Says*. Dad only turned his head to him, and stared Mr. Fred down with a fierce stare on his face. Clenching his teeth, I could have sworn he was about to utter *mothafucka* but he just stared instead.

Dad stared him down soo hard and long without blinking that Mr. Fred looked away. He looked over his shoulder just to see his next-door neighbors Mr. and Mrs. Walker watching the whole thing. They looked as if Mr. Fred was a living ghost.

"Does he really know what he just did?" I could lip read Mrs. Walker saying.

Mr. Fred then looked toward his Buick LaSabre and nervously fumbled his keys, as he struggled to put them in the keyhole because he knew he had spoken out of line. Dad then lit up a Black and Mild, and pulled the clutch of the BMW from reverse to drive as we cruised down the street. We then proceeded into traffic as Scarface *You Don't Hear Me Doe* echoed through Dad's speakers as he stared off into traffic in a world of his own.

I stared outside the window while thinking back to what it was that made Mr. and Mrs. Walker stop having their conversation just to look over and see what would happen next? What did Mr. Fred know about my father that we didn't?

There was something about our dad that made me second guess if driving trucks was all he *really* did for a living. Like at times when my brother and I went to the meat packing house on Malcolm X Boulevard, and how our or order would already be ready, and sat aside for us no matter how busy it was in the store.

Our first cousin Ronnie was always in the streets robbing banks and stealing cars from the better side of town for drug dealers. He was getting into shootouts and robbing banks with dudes who were already out of school. Ronnie would even go as far as to bring my dad back merchandise from rip offs he had done. He would bring my dad back boxes of Black and

Mild cigarettes, Sunday papers, and colognes for my brother and I. One evening Donell asked Ronnie what secret he knew about our dad that we didn't. Ronnie just stared off into space and said-

"Your pops is *the man*."

"Believe me when I tell you.…. He keep's people in line."

As we turned into the parking lot, pedestrians were coming and going from the liquor store, while players were trying to spit their game at the women making their way about. Shade covered the entire pavement when dad turned the music down and took off his Ray Ban sunglasses.

"Wait here and watch the car okay." Dad instructed Donell.

"You got it."

"What did you want out of here by the way?"

"Uhmm . . . The NWA Straight Outta Compton."

"Alright this is how it's going to go," Dad said turning to me pointing his index finger.

"I'm going to do all the talking. You only talk when I nod in your direction giving you the okay."

"Alright then,"

I had never seen our dad straighten someone out in person. Up until now, I had just heard of neighbors referring to Donell and myself as *Big Dave sons*. I even heard Ronnie talking about our dad as if he was as a tough gangster on the *down low*.

As soon as dad opened his car door, and placed one leg on the pavement while slowly rising to his feet, a dude wearing a leather trench coat noticed him. Appearing to be my dads' age, the joy that came over him reminded me of a little kid. He was very sharply dressed, as he had a perfectly shaped afro, shining jewelry and some sharp brown alligator dress shoes.

"My main man, Big Dave," he said holding both his arms in the air.

"Sammie, what's going on with you nowadays?"

"Shit brotha I can't call it, just trying to take care of me and mines."

"Gimme one of your men at this entrance for fifteen minutes."

While watching Sammie instruct the older guy to stand by the double entry burglar bar glass doors, I looked at my dad while he finished his Black and Mild like the world waited on him. Then I looked toward the ongoing rush hour traffic and realized something that would stick with me for the rest of my life.

There's always something going on at all times, the question is if you're a part of it.

O'SHUN M JONES

Dad then nodded in Mr. James direction for me to follow. As the door flew open, dad strolled into Mr. James shop very relaxed and swiftly as if he'd done this a hundred times already.

"Big Dave, I haven't seen you around here in a while." Mr. James said while standing beside a CD case stocking CD's with a fake smile. As Dad walked and stood beside Mr. James, dad began talking very sternly as he had his feet planted behind Mr. James, to the point where I could easily see that my dad was bracing himself for something about to take place.

"James you know it's who I came in here with that's the sole reason I'm even in this shit and sugar record shop."

"Oh . . . well, I remember speaking with Barry earlier today."

Just as soon as Mr. James finished his sentence, my dad jerked his right shoulder back forcing Mr. James to turn around backwards face first into a fist full of brass knuckles my dad wore.

Wam Wam . . . Two quick jabs in the nose threw Mr. James back against the CD stand causing me to jerk back in shock and look around to see if anyone else seen what had just happen, let alone who else was in the shop. Throwing his hands up, as if he were being held up in a robbery, my dad held his afro before viciously upper cutting Mr. James sending him to his knees.

Spitting blood out his mouth and wiping his nose, Mr. James looked up stuttering and mumbling.

"Big Dave, I didn't mean anything by it, hell I know who you are and how you roll man!"

Unsympathetic, my Dad took a knee beside Mr. James when he withdrew his .45 caliber pistol out the back of his slacks. Yanking Mr. James head up with a tight grip on his scalp, my Dad never blinked once.

"Now listen mothafucka, how in the hell do you think you know me?"

"Do I ever come by this piece of shit? Have I ever sat down and asked how the fuck you're doing?"

"No Dave, you never have."

BAM! The butt of the gun went straight into Mr. James' left eye. My dad then shoved Mr. James head toward the floor.

"Come on Dave, I didn't mean nothing by it, please don't shoot me."

As my dad rose up taking deep breaths, he then raised his right foot behind him as if he was about to kick a field goal before taking aim at Mr. James rib cage.

"Awwwwwe!"

"Oh now you didn't mean nothing by it!"

"Well what the hell did you mean by saying *if you was his daddy?*"

"What mothafucker? Now's your chance to speak!"

"Da Dave!"

With the barrel of the magnum .45 in his mouth, all I could think at this point was if dad was actually going to kill this man.

"Every time my sons or nephew come in here, you better give them a store credit. And if you want them to pay, just know I will pay you another visit *and* I'm going to add *you* to my list of mothafuckers to tax!"

"Get the damn CD," Dad said coldly snapping me out a trance.

"Nigga *now* you know me, and next time the wind blows me in here, you're going to owe me." My dad said staring into Mr. James eyes.

"Let's go son."

Chapter 3

Cold Nights and Empty Skies

*"... But I ain't never crossed a man that didn't deserve it
Me be treated like a punk, you know that's unheard of..."*
                                   Coolio—Gangster Paradise

*" ... All this stuff doesn't mean anything, money, this doesn't mean
anything without trust. I have to be able to trust you with my life."*
                                   Robert De Niro—Casino (Film)

Ronnie

SEATED ON THE hood of Al's Lexus facing Martin Luther King Street, I couldn't help but think of the life I was born into.
When it rains it pours.
Hell, I was only seven-teen and my only parent to my knowledge was a base head. Having a base head for a mother was downright embarrassing no matter how you looked at it. Older cats in the neighborhood would ask me about her whereabouts all the time simply because we favored one another, especially one cat named Eddie B.

"Ronnie man where's your moms, my dear friend Deborah?"

He would say with a sly grin on his face as if he knew something I didn't.

The questions they asked often aggravated me because I didn't know if they wanted her to turn a trick, or if they wanted my mom to snort some of their drugs as if she was some sort of crack dummy.

My mom may have done and been called a bunch of things but she sure wasn't no dummy. All around our apartment, buried inside of dictionaries and encyclopedias, she kept old report cards. All of my Mom's old report cards from high school to college were all A's. I just couldn't put together how she up and started *freebasing* and turning tricks for drugs. Hell, she messed both of our lifestyles up the more she chose to be a damn junkie, living a life in need of a fix every minute of the day.

Sometimes I wondered if my pops left my mom before or after she got hooked on heroin? Or if he was the one that hooked her on the drugs? There were a lot of things I wondered about him, and as I grew older never seeing him come around-—the more I hated him.

I hated how I had to grow up in the ghetto, without a choice. Everything my mom brought home was second hand straight from Goodwill. Not having anything made me want everything I seen that looked nice. After years of running the streets as a solider for this and that drug dealer, I wanted respect more than anything.

My best friend JD was down to ride with me no matter what. We believed it was us against the world. We were some outlaws and I knew quite a few other cats that felt the same way. As I looked across the street I couldn't ignore the fact that Uncle Dave was in control of the underworld scene.

Uncle Dave had the drop on all those fools. He knew when the trains of retail merchandise were coming through town, the big bank truck deliveries as well as a few political spokesmen. Uncle Dave knew exactly where to go and bring back enough muscle to pull off a heist, or enough guns to go to war. And most importantly, he had the connection that made the whole city tick, the cocaine connection.

"See any fucking local hustler can make some money, get a crew and run some shit. Old Apache Indian ass mothafuckas, but a Boss is in control at all times."

I could recall Uncle Dave telling me one day outside the pool hall on the east side of town. That's why you had to say *big* in front of his name. When Uncle Dave pulled a job off, he hit it off big.

Barry

I knew it was only a matter of time as to when the tables would turn from me finding myself in the middle of a sticky situation, to actually being a part of some serious shit.

I thought to myself riding in the passenger seat of Ronnie Caprice. Ronnie had just did a paid for murder on behalf of Pee Wee, a high rolling cocaine dealer who was robbed for seventy-five grand and two nine-millimeter pistols with silencers. Once Pee Wee knew who had done it, he brought the proposal to Ronnie.

After casing the dudes and studying how they moved, Ronnie was just like clockwork as to how one week later he finally took them out.

What started out as people daring him to do some wild stuff ended up with people not even daring him at all, because he was down to do whatever to just about anyone. Ronnie was known to do anything from holding drug dealers at gunpoint for their money to being a bodyguard for hire for someone that had a weak reputation. Ronnie held his own weight and reputation in the streets to be as young as he was.

Pulling up alongside some apartments, I parked at a house near a warehouse as Ronnie got out alone with a backpack in hand.

Deep in thought, I leaned up against the driver side door still thinking about the conversation we just had before he had gotten out.

"Look man—"

"I don't need to know these dudes or how the game goes to know that you're walking up in his place with seventy five thousand is not smart at all."

"Since you already put the work in, how bout you bring him back to the parking lot so both of ya'll can get what ya'll want?"

"You're worth more to him if you keep what he really wants and bring him out here to the car."

"Yeah . . . Yeah, you got a point there."

After one song played into another, I was growing more and more impatient waiting in the car.

Something just isn't right. He should have been back if this dude was expecting him.

Cranking the car up, I slowly crept through the projects undetected. Driving toward the apartment unit I remembered seeing Ronnie disappear in, I heard gunshots—then I heard three more shots fired quickly. Once I parked the car, I got out to get a better view of the apartment unit that the noise was coming from. It was then when I seen a short man wearing a muscle shirt quickly shoot from behind a door, running from someone with a black hoody on their head with a gun in their hand.

Slowly jogging away from the car at a safe distance, I ran at an angle from the two so I could remain somewhat inconspicuous. Seeing it was Ronnie chasing Pee Wee, I then took a shortcut behind the apartments to an alley.

Seeing that I was there first, it wasn't long before Pee Wee sprinted around the corner with his hand on his waist, slowing down to withdraw a pistol. Ronnie was still behind him at the same distance he was when I first seem him trailing in the parking lot.

As I watched Pee Wee withdraw his gun and kneel down behind an old couch, I could tell that Ronnie knew he was walking into a trap as I heard his feet come to an abrupt halt on the gravel pavement. Leaning back against the wall in the dark, I still had a clear view as I remained quiet and observed Pee Wee from a distance. Ronnie shadow shrunk smaller the closer he got. Withdrawing my dad's 454 revolver, I held it tightly as I stepped forward to Pee Wee from behind.

Am I actually about to shoot this dude? I got to, I aint got no choice.
BAP BAP!

The shots rang out sounding louder than ever as I squeezed the trigger twice with my arms stretched out in front of me. I braced myself for the kickback watching Pee Wee grab his shoulder and slowly turn around to face me.

BAP BAP!

I left off two more shots into his chest. He stared into my eyes as if I was a ghost, before dropping his pistol and falling knee first onto his side. His glass eyes remained wide open, with a look I'd never seen before.

I jumped at the weight that was forced on my shoulder only to see it was Ronnie that walked up behind me.

"Come on cuz."

"Let's go home before someone sees us," he said with one arm over my shoulder with his gun by his side.

Chapter 4

A Reality Check . . .

"Cash rules ever thang around me, cream get the money, dollar dollar bill ya'll . . . ."   Wu-Tang Clan—Enter the Wu-Tang (36 Chambers)

Barry

"AWWWE COME ON and deal the motherfuckin cards Dave." Uncle Billy spit at dad while he took his time mixing them up for another game of spades.

Friday nights were always when my dad, mom and Uncle Billy would come over to our house and play cards. Mom's sister, Deborah, always said she would come over but she never did.

Uncle Billy was our Dad's most trusted friend. I sometime watched the two of them agree on matters without even speaking. Uncle Billy was the owner of a small club.

The nightmares I was having became more of an ordinary thing because I was having them more so on the regular. I tried my hardest to block out the images with other thoughts, but the look in Pee Wee eyes wouldn't go away.

Two weeks had past, and at first, I was shook up about the whole thing and thought it would be traced back to me, but Ronnie took the whole situation lightly as if he was immune to seeing death.

"We're surrounded by dead men everyday Barry. Some people are just living on their knees until they're put into the casket ya know?"

I hadn't told anyone, especially my dad. However, sometimes, my dad would just stand and stare at me as if he knew I was different, but he couldn't quite name it.

As my graduation grew closer in the spring of '93, so did other things I grew wiser too. Such as how often our mom would be going to and from the Galleria buying expensive purses and jewelry, while dad would be traveling out of town more and more. I once seen our dad come in at two o'clock on a Saturday morning and was dressed in all black. It was odd because he even had a black ski mask in his back pocket.

I knew my dad cared about my brother and me playing sports and how we were performing in them, but he rarely attended our games. Not to mention that Donell was the only Junior on the Varsity basketball team scoring double- doubles and leading scorer in Dallas. I didn't know what to think of our dad but I didn't have to think twice anymore about whether or not he was evolved in other things—things he thought Donnie and I didn't know of.

Over time, I had come to learn more about Uncle Billy's ballroom, *Silks*. Silk's was very popular among those in the street life. Billy had to be the best example of a host I'd ever seen.

Uncle Billy could make anyone laugh and show everybody a good time. Moreover, with the pool tables, food, liquor and live music at his club—people definitely had a good time. But what really brought Billy's club to the top were the dancers he had and the private rooms in the back.

These women would draw in the politicians, lawyers, business owners and police officers. You name it and Billy had access to them. They all were indebted to Billy because of his linear *meeting rooms*. Whether it was for a dance or meeting that you didn't want people to know about, you could come here and no one would know of it. That's why Uncle Billy had a back entrance that led directly upstairs.

And these meetings are where my dad came in at; he would make sure messages were sent, and every massage was delivered physically. Dad *was* the ear to the street. He was that *little birdie* in the sky that could tell you ahead of time if someone was about to get knocked, robbed or if something was bound to come into the city for a very low price.

I put two and two together one Thursday night when I walked back to our house while mom was supposedly at work. Dad was supposed to be out of town with some friends, but the dining room light was lit and his seven series BMW was parked in the driveway.

When I put my key into the lock and twisted it, it didn't budge because the top lock was locked as well. Then I heard—

"Who is it?" The music playing in the background slowly softened until it was completely muted.

"Barry, I left some stuff in my room and I came back to get it."

As Marvin Gaye *I Heard It Through the Grapevine* echoed from the living room throughout the house, I laid eyes on the most money I had ever seen in my life. The first thing I seen were piles of neatly stacked crisp dollar bills spread all over the kitchen table. He had three rows of hundred dollar bills, two rows of fifty dollar bills and three close together rows of twenty dollar bills. Our dad even had two money counting machines on top of the kitchen counter. Smoking a Black and Mild, he seemed to be totally relaxed with my brother and me bearing witness to all the money in his possession. There was even a tub sized three feet high block of money sealed in a see through plastic bag as if it came from a vault.

"Some recruiters came to see me last night after the game daddy," I said with Donell on my heels.

"Yea, I spoke with one of them on the phone and told them that you were going to play yesterday—so what did they offer you?" He said hutched over in the kitchen chair twisting his wrist as if he was trying to regain the feeling in it.

"They said they would give me a full ride."

"There ain't no such thing as a free ride son. They want you to go up there and play hard, win games.

"Well, I'm going to do it pops, I want to make it to the pro's and live the American dream."

Leaving out the house, our dad followed us onto the porch and mocked how my brother showboated during the game he seen him play in.

"I want to see you do that Barry, you and your brother- I want ya'll to live the American Dream," he said taking the Black and Mild out his mouth.

"Just remember, the American Dream is what you make it, not what you think it is."

Chapter 5

Collecting Your Bones

"It's about the rules, the parameters. You take the beating for the friend, you don't betray who you are, what you are . . ."
—John Gotti (Film)

Ronnie

ON A STORMY night during the high school spring break, everything was going to pay off big time for my crew and me. Although the weather was pouring down raining, that wasn't going to stop our plan from going into full swing.

After some advice from Barry and Donell, I changed up my whole operation in terms of how I went about robbing drug dealers. Juice, a big time cocaine dealer, was the hustler my crew and I were going after. He had a drug house on our side of town, the Southside and thought he was too big to pay up.

What he failed to realize was that he was big and feared on his side of town, but once he came to my hood, he was in a totally different world. Once I hit the age of seventeen, I had older players in the palms of my hand. There was a long list of established hustlers that feared me and the people within my circle. When we hit you, we overdid everything.

We put the word out that if you weren't from our hood, then *you* and *your whole* crew would be at risk. Risk of getting your drug house shot up, runners getting robbed or Lieutenant's robbed during a delivery unless we were cut in on it. The main drug dealer in the city was Big John. He took a liking to me and my crew because we stayed out his way as well as handled all his beefs.

I mean these dudes just didn't get it. You pay rent on the house and the turf. We sent neutral warnings by sticking up a couple of the runners they had, and we shot at their cars when we seen them making deliveries, but they wouldn't budge.

As I filled the clips into the machine guns and loaded the shells in the shotgun, I felt an adrenaline rush. I felt as though I was made to shake hustlers and bank tellers down, it just gave me a rush.

At times, I felt as though I was the Grim Reaper. Yeah my cousins were moving on to bigger stakes, and so was I. Barry was going to college on a full athletic scholarship. While Donell on the other hand, was going on to start as a Point Guard in this years' McDonald's All American high school basketball team. But me, I was going to be a legend—I was going to be a street legend.

Soon as the skies were blanketed with blackness, Cap and I walked down the street to Juice house. We walked to the house on opposite sides of the street from one another so we could cover each other in case we were spotted. I walked, then crawled onto Juice front lawn before laying beneath the bushes with my shotgun.

"Always look them in the eye before you kill'em."

Time slowly passed by as we all laid hidden like chameleons. Just as we expected from watching their routine the workers left out the house to go do deliveries and get some food, while in the meantime there would only be just one Lieutenant and a doorman in the house.

Those two would be the only ones in the house when Juice would come and deliver the drugs for the weekend, while at the same time picking up monies made from the week prior.

Cap lay in the bushes across from mines. I could tell he was growing bored by his nodding off. I snapped my fingers at him and whispered to him.

"Hey, hey Cap."

"Wake up shit, put your damn mask on nigga."

It was around eleven twenty when I seen the Chevrolet Tahoe on chrome rims waiting to turn onto the street with the blinkers blinking.

"Pssssss, psssss." I heard JD signaling to us to get our attention. As the Tahoe slowly pulled alongside the curb, we heard people moving around from within the inside of the house. From the sound of the voices, it was only two people. Then the next chain of events came almost like second nature.

As the locks on the front door turned, the burglar bar door slowly squealed from the old hinges as it opened. Juice then stepped out of his truck.

"What's up big homie?" Lil Ron said while standing on the porch.

"What ya'll niggas looking like in there?"

"We're sold out, and we counted the money twice so it's a cool fifty grand we got."

"Man this neighborhood be rolling hard." Lil Ron said grinning as if he couldn't believe the amount of profit they were making.

The moment Juice attempted to put his foot on the porch step to shake Lil Rons' hand, I signaled for the others to come out of hiding. JD then jumped the porch rail darting through the open door that Lil Ron had left halfway open.

BOOOOM!

The twelve gauge sounded off as I turned to my left to blow Lil Ron into the wall. JD distracted my aim as I got a clean shoulder shot while aiming for Lil Ron's head. Juice froze during the ambush while reaching for his gun. Aiming to fire again and finish Ron off for good, I turned my head slightly seeing Benny swiftly step inside the house firing off automatic rounds into the walls hitting everything in sight with his assault rifle.

BOOOOM!

The second shot sounded off as I fired blowing away Rons' whole knee while making a bloody mess in the process.

"Don't even try it mothafucka!" Cap yell at Juice with his index finger on the trigger of the Mack 11.

BAT BAT BAT!!

The shots rang out in semi-automatic mode.

Painfully backing back hunched forward grabbing his abdomen, I stepped forward turning the handle grip of the shotgun toward his head swiping his temple.

"Run yo ass back to yo side of town, cause this side is ours!" I heard JD yelling out from the back of the house as I heard footsteps matching the pace of Maurice Green in a track race.

I knocked the air out of Juice by shoving the shotgun into his stomach where the gunshot wound was, before he quickly fell down.

"Cap... Check the car!"

WAM WAM!

The butt of my shotgun echoed from drumming Juice in the face while his head bounced off the concrete. Juice had to have been in his mid thirties, and I figured that was why he didn't take my crew and I serious at first—because we were all some youngsters.

"You don't know who you're fucking with!" I said through clenched teeth while breathing heavily still dropping blows with my fist into his nose.

JD followed by Benny rushing out from the house behind me toward the car that Pookie awaited in with a backpack his hand. The only thought on my mind was beating Juice to a pulp, then shooting him on his yard. Cap held a duffle bag in his hand, giving me the thumbs up letting me know that he had just found some goods and now he was headed to the getaway car.

HONK HONK!

Pookie sounded the horn signaling for me to come on while swerving the car closer to my side of the sidewalk. With the trunk of the car to the main street, we would have to use the back streets as a getaway now since we all could hear the police sirens.

Rising to my feet, I grabbed the shotgun standing over Juice holding the barrel to his forehead. I then squeezed the trigger and realized that I fired all the shells I had loaded as I pulled back a blank.

"Damn mothafucka!" Headed toward the getaway car, I threw the shotgun toward the car and JD reached down to pick it up before placing it inside.

I then signaled for them to drive to the alley to pick me up behind the houses. As they drove off and around the block, I saw the first cop car on the scene turn wildly onto the street racing toward me. It was then when I realized that they would follow me to the getaway car if I ran behind the houses.

"Damn . . . Fuck man!"

Running in the opposite direction, I ran two blocks over and was cornered by Dallas Police Department squad cars.

"Put your hands behind your head!" The cops yelled at me holding their barrettes at me as if they would rather shoot me than wait and see what I would do next.

"Don't move! Ten four, we have one purp in sight now!"

"There's three more, did you see them as well?" The voice yelled over the dispatch radio.

As I lay over the hood of the car being read my rights, I saw the neighbors that lived in the houses that I ran past. Some school kids and older people looked on at me as if I was a hoodlum.

I then thought about my father not being there for me, when I really needed him. And how long I've been a soldier in the neighborhood, but now I was official. After word got out in the city that I had knocked off Juice, I would be respected by everyone that crossed my path. As my thoughts faded into one after the other, I observed how slow the traffic had been moving filled with people being nosey to see what had taken place for there to be so many police cars.

Then I noticed a burgundy station wagon, driving at a snail's pace while the passengers looked on in disbelief as if they couldn't believe their eyes. JD rode in the passenger seat while Pookie stared straightforward hoping not to get pulled over to the side.

JD nodded at me without blinking as I was thrown in the back seat of the squad car.

While I rode in silence, irritated and in deep thought, I was already mentally preparing myself to handle what I was walking into now, another shit whole situation.

As the two fat white officers drove through the city making small talk among themselves as if I wasn't in the car, I could tell they cared less about where my parents were.

"Turn that up Jimmy."

"*Today marks the second day the bank robbers are at large in the City Of Dallas. . . . . On Wednesday morning approximately 8:20 a.m., the Guaranty Bank was robbed by three masked men carrying machine guns and assault rifles. Policemen on duty within the bank said they were very organized. Already having a very thorough understanding and knowledge of just where to go, what time to do it and how much they expected to leave with as they took over the bank floor, offices and cash vault.*"

Then I heard the on duty police officer speaking on everything that took place.

"*There were two Spanish men and one black man. The black man was giving the orders and was very relaxed about the whole thing, forceful, but relaxed.*"

From there, the anchor lady came back on the air only to give a final report about the robbery.

"*The three masked bank robbers are said to have gotten away with over $575,000 in unmarked bills just minutes before the security truck was scheduled to make its pickup in route to the Guaranty Headquarters. Authorities are saying that it had to be an inside job . . .*"

"Can you believe that shit Jimmy, hell a tenth of that would do me some real good right about now," he said sipping his coffee looking out into traffic.

Chapter 6

All Grown Up Now

"Now its time for me to make my impression felt so sit back relax and strap on your seatbelt . . . You never been on a ride like this before . . ." Dr. Dre—The Chronic Album

3 Years Later . . . .

Barry

BOY OH BOY has time flown by since I came to North Carolina in the fall of '93. A lot of things have changed in my life since I've arrived here. Among my *sideline* engagements, I had been playing football for a while on the verge of graduating with a degree in Business.

I really liked all the little things I learned from my major and how an enterprise was ran. At times, I felt as though I wanted to be a famous business mogul just as much as I wanted to be in the NFL.

My brother on the other hand was a junior at Paul Quinn College and the leading scorer in the state. Pops and I were proud of Donell and how this was his second consecutive year leading the state in scoring, not to mention he had the most games played ending with a triple—double. Through Donell's acquired fame on the basketball court, he had become quite the talk of the city since I had left.

"Man if you want to know what's going on back home, then look no further bro."

"I can't be touched on the court bro. I'm like Magic Johnson on the black top." He would brag with excitement.

"At the *Hoop It Up* tournaments bro, people be shouting *The Big O* out on the court man . . . I ball on them dudes like Oscar Robertson," Donell said before switching the subject.

"You heard of that dude Kevin Garnett getting drafted B?"

"Uhmm, yeah. Isn't that the skinny kid from Chicago that you said was tall as hell?"

"Hell yeah. That's him . . . Well he got drafted by the Timberwolves."

"I'm not knocking the man because he made it, but next time I get a chance to make it *big time*, I'm going to take the opportunity by all means necessary and run with it."

Donell didn't have to say it for me to realize how much he thought about all the stats he had put up throughout college only to watch others get drafted into the NBA. Even Ronnie once wrote me telling me that Donell expressed how frustrated he was with not being drafted already and at times, he regretted his decision of going to college.

At the same time, I knew my brother and I knew that it wasn't just the thrill of the game that drove him- but the attention, the fact that all eyes were on him all throughout the game.

"Pops is a *made man* bro, these street hustlers respect him," Donell said after a moment of silence between us.

"Oh yeah?"

"Every since Ronnie beat that hustler Juice into a coma, dudes that aren't from round here don't come round here."

When Ronnie went to the jail some years back, around the same time when I graduated, his crew became larger than life by making dudes in the street life live in fear for their lives.

Ronnie had been locked up since we graduated and was eligible for parole in another year and a half. Although he was still in his mentality of being a mobster, I could tell from our brief conversations that he was changing mentally to say the least.

He now was more concerned about me and Donell's wellbeing. Ronnie often asked about what we had been up to and with everything I was doing after school, he would always warn me to watch myself and to be careful. Since I'd been in college, I had been to bike week in Myrtle Beach, Freak Nik in Atlanta and even Memorial Day weekend in Miami.

And after seeing all that action in those cities, I was able to visualize myself *way* beyond the city limits of my small city. Around this time I met my girlfriend Brandi who I had grown quite fond of specifically because of our mutual interest. We both had dreams of running a famous company, not to mention she was a stellar chess player, which made me admire the way she thought things through as I did myself. After seeing what I did day in and day out, she'd ask me from time to time-

"Barry you're a genuine guy and that's what I love about you. But I just don't understand why you choose to do what it is you do."

Since the second semester of my freshman year, I had been going to Fayetteville, N.C doing my own thing making fast money. It all started one weekend when some friends and I went to *Jazzy T's* gentlemen club in Atlanta where I met two brothers from Chicago.

These dudes were the real reason why I was able to stay rolling in cash while away from home. Des and Jr. transported drugs from Florida to Georgia and up to as far as Connecticut. These brothers really had their operations *down packed* and brought me into the *game* as far as doing things on a larger scale went.

Nowadays, Des and Jr. mainly took a liking to me because they could trust me. Des and Jr weren't leveled headed and often made costly mistakes due to their short temper.

As time passed from being involved with them, I found myself centered around people that were involved in the underworld sort of speak. Des and Jr. had built a reputation of violence with the hustlers they dealt with. People would often call me as a last resort all hours in the night.

"B . . . My nigga. I swear on every dollar in my pocket I'm going to smoke them niggas, and I ain't gonna think twice about it."

Even though the brothers had their hustle going on long before they met me, time after time, I was the one smoothing things out and persuading hustlers to pay Des and Jr. This led me to knowing dealers and mobsters firsthand who were from all over the south and Midwest.

Chapter 7

My Gut Instinct

"Don't let yourself get attached to anything you are not willing to walk out on in 30 seconds flat if you feel the heat around the corner."
— Robert De Niro-Heat (Film)

"YEAH YEAH, NONE of these dudes are untouchable you know?" Dave told Melvin on the phone in regards to their last out of town job they had done.

Super Bowl XXVII proved to be just another come up as Melvin, Duke and himself went to Pasadena, California and robbed the city dry leaving with over half a million dollars in cash—not to mention jewelry appraised at another half a million dollars.

Back in Dallas, the jewelry wouldn't be hard to fence being that Billy was the go to guy to in order to fence hot items.

After all these years as a truck driver, the company truck made it easy to slip under the police radar. With Carlos being the leader of the Mexican Cartel and a long time friend, Billy and I would sell drugs for him from time to time due to the fact that we were all so close and tight.

Having fifty kilos of cocaine in my trailer in exchange for seven hundred and fifty thousand dollars was nothing out the ordinary. I was getting three grand per kilo for delivering them meaning I would pull down one hundred and fifty grand off this deal alone. But this delay wasn't like my usual way of doing business.

Usually I would meet up with whoever I had already talked to on the phone and it would be a fast exchange. It was always done outside in the open, face to face and with no one else around.

But by this dude being late and drawing attention to himself with the loud music he was blasting was more than out the ordinary—I felt iffy at that moment.

I had been doing this same routine for years and every time I met with someone they would pull up to my truck, staring at me in my eyes but not this dude, he drove past me.

"What in the hell is this punk ass mothafucka doing?"

I thought as I stood halfway in-between my truck and another trailer feeling out of my element.

"Something just isn't right."

I waived him over to me with one hand and kept the other on my revolver in my coat pocket.

"*I may have to kill this young ass nigga.*"

"Yo you Billys' man with the coke right?"

As he walked in-between my trailer, I withdrew my revolver and rested in on my leg discretely while I leaned against my trailer.

"Yo man, you suppose to give me the drugs and shit in the open."

He said with his hands resting on his waist as if he was tired. That's when I saw the unmarked sedan with tinted windows drive by slowly at a distance that was suspicious to me.

Immediately I slung my revolver upside the dude's temple, wrapped my hands around his neck and inserted my gun into his mouth.

"You want me to blow yo stupid ass brains out on the curb?"

"Yo young ass call ya'self setting me up?"

I had him cornered just as much as he had me. This time when I looked over my shoulder, I seen another unmarked car parked at a standstill with a clear view of both of us standing in—between the trailers.

As I rushed him to the back of my trailer to get out of the eyesight of the onlookers, I threw him off me and up against my trailer. When he flew backwards reaching for leverage, I caught a glimpse of the shiny brass badge on his belt holster.

My heart jumped into my throat as I realized it was already too late after I pulled back the hair trigger.

BOOM BOOM!

The revolver sounded off as one round went into his forehead and into his neck.

When I ran toward the wooded area, I heard squad cars skid and take off in a fast response to the shots fired. I then heard a helicopter hovering somewhere in the vicinity around the same time the officers began yelling.

"Put the gun down now and put your hands in the air!"

"Stand still and get on your knees!"

The DEA and ATF agents screamed aiming their guns at me as if they were marksman shooters.

As I got on one knee at a time, all I could think about was me second-guessing my gut instinct. When I was being read my rights, I contemplated on whether or not the officers would take a bribe. I had done dozen times before and I knew I had access to the money but after killing one of their own, I knew it wouldn't happen.

Special Agent Logan & 1st Grade Detective Johnson

"Now you see exactly what you're getting yourself into Det. Johnson."

Special Agent Logan told Detective Johnson who sat in the passenger seat of the unmarked squad car.

"Just like *Big* Dave McCoy, there are even more ruthless criminals out here who have zero tolerance for law enforcement, especially undercover informants."

Mike Millan was the rookie undercover who Dave had just murdered. Millan and Det. Johnson had recently graduated from the police academy together. Johnson and Millan were close friends and had been following Dave, as well as several other mid level profile gangsters from Texas for quite some time.

"That shit isn't right Logan."

"Well, it's up to people like me and you along with reliable source to make it right. With the help of federal funding we can infiltrate and take down these coldblooded criminals that cause corruption in our society."

"But one thing you must keep in mind at all times Detective." Logan said with his index finger in the air.

"These men aren't just dangerous killers with crooked police on their payroll, but their smart."

"You can't ever, not for one moment underestimate these people who we're going after. You have to realize that the moment you take your mind off the case, you're made. You might as well have exposed yourself with your badge in hand—you hear me?"

"If you don't dedicate yourself to every case, you will be made. If you don't learn these men ,you'll be made. If you slip up at proving yourself one time too many, you're a dead man."

Logan thoroughly expressed the units need for him to remain focused, while at the same time briefing him on cases and investigations that Det.

Johnson would start working on to infiltrate. His first case to assist in investigating was the Gulf Cartel in west Texas.

"Now this investigation has already taken off and it will be *your* job as a Detective to learn these guy's methods of operation in order to make a impact on the next organization we will assign you to."

"Now first things first, you are to learn how these so called *gangsters* secure their drugs during trafficking schemes, okay?"

Logan said to Det. Johnson as they ducked under the caution tape to enter the back of the trailer that Dave was driving.

"Now take notes on everything you see and remember it because there will come a time when you need to prove yourself."

It was then when Det. Johnson realized that his new DEA Division was going to be all work and no play. It was just a matter of time before Det. Johnson would be in so deep that he himself would question if all he had wanted to achieve was even worth it.

Chapter 8

Rags To Riches

"... Its hard for a nigga just to breathe in the streets, let alone trying to make cheese in the streets, niggas bleeding in the streets..."
Trick Daddy ft. Money Mark—Book Of Thugs

Barry

FROM THE OUTSIDE looking in, it may have seemed like I had the weight of the world on my shoulders, but I seen it as I had the world in my hands. The more I went to school, the more I found myself using what I learned in class in the streets.

I was the man now.

I mean I had put away close to six hundred grand these past three years. The illegal money was soo easy to make and at the same time, so much of it to get—that it gave me a rush to be a Boss.

Des and Jr. not only let me run their operations for the summer, but year around when they realized that their clientele had increased. And it was only because dealers felt more at ease when it came to dealing with me instead of them.

By being in complete control, I decided to move Lil Boo, Pat and Joe Joe from Dallas out to North Carolina with me as my enforcers and that's when I began extorting business owners.

The whole time, I didn't even realize how deep I was getting into the game. Then I got news of my pops getting busted with that truck load of drugs. I halfway thought he had a chance still with him having all the connections he had already. But when the whole ordeal made the local papers and news back home that he killed an undercover cop, I knew he wasn't going to get parole. I was saddened to hear of him receiving a natural life sentence, but in—between the phone calls we had, pops opened my eyes up.

"I was all the way out there in the underworld, and you have to realize that it won't last forever. You have to know when you're time is up. Like I used to

tell you in those chess games, just as much as you're watching your surroundings, you have to look after yourself."

Nowadays when we spoke on the phone, he would say encouraging things by telling me to push myself at practice and to not surround myself with the wrong crowd as Donell had so painfully done.

Up until this point, I had centered myself around the most known dealers and goons who depended on me. Whether it was getting one dude out of a bind or allowing someone to pay me on a later date- everyone liked the way I handled business. And in exchange, they were loyal to me.

On the other hand, it seemed that with the rise of my street credibility, my brother's ability to manage his life off the court was taking a toll on him to the extent of him not even having a chance to be drafted after college. When we talked nowadays, I could tell that all the local and media attention was going to his head for better and worse. From missing basketball practices, to having one too many groupies- Donell chances of making it into the NBA was slowly passing him by. What made matters worse was that the schools' athletic program was on the verge of suspension due to theft of the athletic department funds.

While I looked to Bill and Jeff, the offensive coordinators for the Pittsburgh Steelers and Jacksonville Jaguars, they told me that the offer was still on the table as far as getting drafted went. While my brother chances were pretty much shot once he got caught up with Stanley and caught that case making the news all throughout the city.

Ronnie

After three and half years in the joint, with only six more months left, I was more than ready to be out on the streets running a rank on the outside.

I came to learn that from behind these walls, your reputation was already sixty percent of what type of dude you were and your actual muscle was only forty percent.

I decided that now once I got out, I mainly wanted to watch my brothers back, because I didn't want to see them get killed let alone end up in here where I was. It seemed that these days, the real gangsters were locked up and the *phony cronies* were in the *free world* faking and making it.

I felt as though I had seen it all. I had seen some killers on the outside come in here facing twenty and thirty years turn into some rat ass informants.

I'd seen grown men break down and cry like babies because they knew they weren't going to ever step a foot outside these caged fences.

With all the gangster *wannabes* and dudes that weren't built for the street life, I couldn't do nothing but shake my head when I thought about my younger cousin's situation. Ever since the McDonald's High School game, Donell was an acclaimed statewide all star point guard. I would collect all his newspaper articles and pictures with his name attached to it.

Then I got word by way of the news that his athletic scholarship was in jeopardy. It turned out that he was apprehended for riding with Stanley among other friends of his in a car with drugs and drug paraphernalia and was later charged with the intent to distribute. I knew it was just a matter of him being in the wrong place at the wrong time, but I knew he definitely lost his chances of getting drafted with all the negative media attention.

During my bid, I had only gotten four visits from my mother throughout my entire stretch. She would come to visit me like clockwork on my birthday as if that was the only day out of the year when she remembered I existed. I didn't receive any cards, letters or nothing from her.

I wasn't surprised because I knew that she was still strung out on drugs and that was the main reason why she didn't make time for me. I didn't spend much time dwelling on who did and didn't come and see me, but instead I spent more time lifting weights, getting big. Since I had been down, I met some dudes whose reputation was just as strong as mine.

Bodie and Antroine were two inmates that I had met while doing my stretch and was real as they came. I realized this when I stabbed a man to death right beside Bodie and he didn't speak a word of it to anyone. After that, we began to talk about the *hit man* jobs we had done when he mentioned Antroine.

Antroine turned out to be trigger man from New Orleans, who's time was almost up and he reminded me of myself when I was robbing everything moving. Up until I left, the three of us grew close and we knew that we would eventually link up on the *other side*. But the one thing that I was hoping to come to an end sooner or later were the nightmares I was having since I had been here.

In-between having hopes of getting out of here and never coming back, I was having nightmares every night. From all the robberies and murders I had committed, I was seeing those same people faces in my sleep. I was hearing their plea for help in the middle of the night. While some people found drugs in the penitentiary, some found God. And at times, I felt as though these visions and voices were from God telling me that one day all the killing would all have to end.

Chapter 9

Tears and Departures

"They say you can't turn a bad girl good, but once a good girl's goin' bad she's gone forever . . . I'll mourn forever, shit I gotta live with the fact I did you wrong forever"   Jay-Z—Song Cry

Barry

*I*HAD IT all as my senior year at A& T came to an end. I was having plenty of sex, driving the newest of convertible cars and making more and more money everyday literally.

I had connections with hustlers outside the state that I was supplying with bails of cocaine, heroin and pounds of marijuana.

This shit is too damn easy.

I thought riding thinking back to how my graduation was only a few months away and how I had already put away my first million dollars. I couldn't help but nod my head while listening to the chorus of *Dr. Dre Ring Ding Dong* when I thought how everything was playing.

Kingston and Blue were my right hand men. The drugs we smuggled in from the Port Of Miami were better than Des and Jr ever scored and twice as cheap. I *was* the connect and I had the whole operation running like clockwork.

After witnessing how I moved and handled myself, Brandi couldn't help but be turned out. She was fascinated at how much power I had. She never questioned me nor tried to use me for the money she could tell I was making. I slowly began to trust her because Brandi would always come through for me no matter what.

As time progressed, my teammates were growing jealous of me due to my fame in the street life, which made it hard to be the teams' offensive team Captain. I didn't let that bother me because I had things that my teammates didn't have. I was twenty-three with my own four bedroom house and condominium across town. I had four cars and two trucks that were all brand new.

My dad had been sending me letters time and time again telling me to focus on sports and learn from my brothers' mistake, but I slowly stop replying. I wasn't the same naive son that I left home as. I was waist deep into the *trap* life.

Lately, Brandi and I had been getting into arguments more often than usual. She seemed to be having what I felt at the time were mood swings. I figured she would as it grew closer for me to graduate and leave school meaning we would either break up or stay together. Although I knew I had some serious decision making to do, I was leaning more to playing pro football until I was injured at practice.

This is what I get for not having my head in the game.

I said aloud frustrated while lying on the doctor's table holding ice on my knee. All I could think about was how in the hell did this shit happen to me.

"Well Barry, your ACL is torn in two."

Tuning him out as he continued talking, I just stared at the ceiling as what he said went in one ear and out the other.

Those recruiters aren't checking for a player on the bench especially when you have eleven ready and physically fit players ready to work hard now.

As weeks turned into the last two months when graduation came in May, I couldn't have been pulled into more directions. From Des and Jr. steady questioning me on what I was going to do after graduation, to all the hustlers I meet from in the street that would rather do business with me than Des and Jr—to Brandi nagging about spending more time together.

My mother was overjoyed to see me graduate. She was taking pictures and crying, not to mention that Donell was happy for me too. Everyone spirits were high to see me graduate, but I was dying on the inside. Not only had my NFL contacts stopped answering and returning my calls, but a few even changed their number.

Brandi, on the other hand, was beginning to throw up a little too often as she would make frequent trips in and out of the hospital. She later would tell me that she felt fine and that it was something she ate. I had too much going on myself to really sweat her and her unbalanced emotions.

Donell and I finally got some time alone when he went on to tell me of his plans to start as the Point Guard for SMU. The more he talked to me, I realized he wasn't really focused on school.

"Bro, the more I play in these street tournaments, the more these dudes want to party. It's like every since I had that *run in* with the police, people actually expect me to have drugs for sale now."

Donell said smoking a joint, while at the same time cracking a smile as if he had stumbled upon a gold mine.

"Oh so you're dealing now lil bro?"

"Shit, bro this shit pays and they can't pay me enough."

"It sounds like you're getting distracted?"

"Shit, I'm not getting distracted, I'm getting paid. Hell, my bills aren't going to pay themselves."

"Plus, I got fired two weeks ago because the company laying people off."

"Borden?"

"Since when does a milk company business get slow?"

"Man I'm not making money hand over fist like you are, but until I get back into school, this shit is my homework. I mean I already got the clientele bro. I got these niggas that's dealing full time under my thumb too because I got the best shit,"

"The average hustler out here dope has been stepped on more than a few times before they get it into their hands. I got the drop on all these dudes Barry."

Right then it didn't hit me, but as time passed I felt as though his words grabbed hold of me and his words played over and over in my head.

When I woke up this morning, Brandi was already up cooking a full breakfast as she did every morning we spent the night together. She knew I had an early flight to catch back to Dallas and she was on pens and needles not knowing if I was going to come back or not. I knew her head was all over the place when she began to refer to us as *a family* like it was something different all of a sudden.

I still had hopes of getting drafted into the NFL by way of playing arena football first and there was no way I could do that by having a woman. I learned from Des and Jr. that women wanted two things, time or money—and if I wanted to put my all into my future, I needed them both. I withdrew my luggage out the trunk and hugged Brandi tightly for what seemed like forever, which really was the last time.

"Are you coming back for me Barry?" She said staring into my eyes with my face in-between her hands.

"I can't guarantee that right now, I got tryouts with the SaberCats in California. I got to get back in shape for practice."

"So when am I going to see you again?" She said trying to hold back tears in her glassy eyes.

"Uhmm . . . Well, we got tryouts, then a scrimmage game. After that I'm plan on catching up with some old friends back home."

"I'll make sure we stay in touch though," I said as I started walking away from her at the same time.

With every step I took, I thought of every thought I planted into her head about the future that we would share together. Going through the metal detectors, I glanced back one last time only to see her sitting in a chair sobbing, while covering up her facial expression and holding her stomach with a stream of tears falling from her face. I realized that there wasn't anything I could say to change the fact that I had to do what I had to do. Little did I know then that I was headed toward a future that was greater than I ever imagined.

Chapter 10

A Vision And A Mission

"... When you're raised up where I come from and to make it out is a blessing, because half the cats where I come from never learn they lesson..." Too Short ft. 8Ball & MJG—Can't Stop Rapping

Barry

AS TIME WENT by, my thoughts of whether or not I'd actually made the team were starting to fade. Nonetheless, my phone continued to ring off the hook with issues happening back in North Carolina. Des and Jr. just couldn't keep things under control. Not one day went by I didn't think about everyone I had meet off in college. Brandi often told me that having a good heart was like a double edge sword.

"Keepin' it real will get you left behind Barry."

"Man word got back and got around quick that you were a Boss in North Carolina," Donell said while staring out into traffic from the passenger side.

"How you figure that bro?"

"Your crew told JD and me over the phone a couple of times already. Hell he showed us the pictures of ya'll at the club all jeweled up, drinking Rozay and whatnot. Hell, I even rode in your Lexus and slept in that *phat* crib you had bro."

"Yeah, we were doing a little something."

"Look bro, there isn't any college dudes out here wearing Presidential Rolex's, and riding in the latest Lexus sedans with two houses in their name. That shit is unheard of. Hell the whole home team is waiting for you to come back down here and do the same thing."

"Shit, so what you think is going to happen? It sounds like you're not even thinking about playing ball anymore."

"I'm just saying,"

"I'm like the G Money in this thing. I already know all the right people and everybody who I don't know already know what I do. These hustlers know me either from playing ball or dealing here and there."

"How about you let me get myself squared away and only if this football thing doesn't work out, I'll put together some things."

Enthusiastic about me not getting accepted into the arena football league, Donell knew I would be a man of my word as he went about getting me hip to all the small and big time hustlers that were dealing around the city. Their problem was that the cities biggest hustler, Big John was charging them too much—only giving older hustlers discounts and taking the younger hustlers turf.

As for as how the whole city operated, Uncle Billie's spot was still were all of the movers and shakers hung out.

"Well well well, if ain't my mothafuckin nephew back in the world again." Uncle Billy said with a smile as wide as Texas on his face.

"Wassup Unc."

"Hell everything I want to be up nephew."

"Let's go somewhere and talk Unc,"

"I can do you one better nephew, let's go out back and talk."

As the door closed behind us and he scanned the back parking lot, Uncle Billy began speaking as if he knew the moment I came home that I would eventually want to get down.

"Now look here nephew, if you're going to get in this game, you got to have your mind up and be willing to take the good with the bad. Now are you down with this shit one hundred percent, because this isn't the Carolinas. The game is bigger than those two states."

"And that's why I want in."

"Okay then . . . Two days from now there will be an armored truck making a routine refueling stop outside of Lufkin County. I want you to get a group of guys and take it out."

"And when you finish that gig—if you want, I got a few banks for ya'll to knock off too. Now, if ya'll do good, there's a lot more jobs to go after . . . I'll provide you the schematics for the banks and the truck route tomorrow nephew."

Over the next few days, Uncle Billy gave me a thorough run down of all the heist he had to offer—the same ones my pops and his crew used to take down.

"Now this shit has been going on long before you went to college, nephew, but since Dave got popped, dudes don't have the nuts to do it anymore. What

I'm trying to tell you is this, it's all about the timing. The sky is the limit young blood, and with the position you're in. . . . Everything is just out there waiting for you."

Toward the end of '97 as Thanksgiving holiday rolled on by, so was I—I was rolling in fast money.

The more I got settled back into the swing of things, I found new up and coming hustlers to bring into my crew. Short Dogg was the first I felt as though I needed to meet up with because he was a young cat with access to a lot of guns.

"He's a young and crazy lil mothafucker. He will shoot anything moving and ask questions later. He thinks he's O Dog from Menace to Society."

I thought to myself about what JD had already told me about the fella, along with what I knew of him already.

As we drove to his side of town he wasn't hard to find being that he was a short, tattooed dude, wearing a Yankee fitted cap.

"JD told me that you would find me sooner or later."

"Yeah man, I wanted us to link up and do business you know?"

"So what business you talking about doing B?"

"Well, I want to buy a lil' something now and then work out the details later on."

"Follow me dog." Short said as he turned around and headed to the trunk of his car.

"Damn, you can get all this Short?" I said admiring his Smith and Wesson M&P 15 equipped with a night vision scope.

"Yeah B, with this here, you can grant any nigga death wish."

Making small talk about how he got his reputation in N.Y.C, we decided to exchange numbers and stay in touch.

"That dude is definitely already established. A connect like him is exactly what we need to stay a step ahead JD."

Chapter 11

Setting A Mark

"Thinking of a master plan . . . . So I start my mission—leave my residence thinking how I could get some dead presidents"
                                                    Rakim—Paid In Full

Barry

EVEN THOUGH DONELL and I formed a team- we all were more like family. The moment I stepped in for Des and Junior operations, the murders stopped. The problem was that they were just so damn hotheaded.

Back home, even though everyone was content with making the money we were already making—I wasn't and I wanted to get in touch with Uncle Billy's cocaine connect, who was also a close friend of our father.

"Yo nephew, this Mexican fella Carlos isn't just someone you can call up on the phone or go looking for without being invited to see already you understand?"

Uncle Billy said while leaning over the bar talking to Donell and I.

"He's a *made* mothfucka. He's down with the Gulf Cartel . . . You know . . . The Mexican Cartel."

"The Cartel . . . So you're saying they smuggle drugs in huh?"

Donell said not knowing how much control and power a Cartel carried.

"Naw young blood."

"I'm saying these dudes are like on some Godfather shit you follow me?"

"They carry machine guns around everywhere. They pat you down before you sit and talk to'em, and once you do all that, they'll still look at you all suspicious and shit." Uncle Billy finished while swallowing a shot of Hennessey straight.

"Now your father Dave was an exception. He and Carlos were in the Army together, somewhere called Fort Hood or something like that."

"Those Mexican mothafuckas loved your pops."

"Oh yeah?" Donell said smiling.

"But I know where to find his people at. They got a mechanic shop on the East side of town. I'll go by there tomorrow and tell them you want to meet with him."

"Give them my cell and pager number too."

"Naw nephew, in this game cell phones don't exist. We do everything face to face."

"Now next line of business is the streets. The streets are talking, and one of them is Big John."

"What about him . . . We don't deal dope…Yet." Donell shot back with a cocky attitude.

"Listen nephew . . . Big John been around since your pops was starting out getting his feet wet in the game. And what ya'll need to realize is that to be the man, you got to beat the man."

Donell

"Man, ya'll niggas sure as hell doing something right if ya'll aren't even selling drugs."

Stanley said admiring Donell's car.

"Naw my nigga, we got our hands on other shit, and our eyes on bigger stakes."

Every since Donell had been selling the merchandise they would steal off trains, he was rolling in more and more money himself. Billy even showed him how to open up his first business, a pawn shop selling all the merchandise they had acquired.

Donell had been waiting for this second chance, his chance at once again being able to shine brighter than the rest, his chance to make it out the hood and be a renowned person. Although he was Barry's younger brother, he had his sights on becoming bigger than Stanley could ever imagine.

Where Stanley and Donell were different at was the fact that Donell paid much more attention to detail. Stanley on the other hand was more focused on the money to be made and not the risk that lay before it—as the time when they were caught with the drugs in his car.

"Man I been hustling all my life, even when you were in college and I'm ready to do it bigger. Big John thinks that the whole city owes him since he's the only one with the *Grade A* shit."

"My cousin Ronnie gets out in a few weeks, and we're going to bring him into this thing we're doing too Stan."

Donell said pulling into the parking lot of Roberts Ready to Wear clothing store.

"Shit, that nigga is a hustler's nightmare. I remember how he had his crew gunning down everything in sight."

"Man, I'm seeing this nigga Eddie B more and more now, is he still a player in the game or what?"

Donell said pointing at Eddie B exit the clothing store with bags.

"Shit something like that, he get high on his own supply though. He's been seen hanging around here and there, but it's nothing major."

"Yea I figured that much. It's just that every time I see that dude, he's always asking how my moms and aunt are doing, but they never speak of him though."

"But yeah… We're going to be official when Ronnie come back home."

Detective Johnson

This whole *Gulf Cartel* assignment was one hell of a challenge. Everyday I was monitoring wiretapped conversations from the Gulf Cartel.

"These are some ruthless motherfuckers."

I often thought to myself while taking notes about the extensive drug smuggling methods they had.

The Gulf Cartel didn't care who got hurt in the process or how many people lives were put at risk to get their dugs into the states. I adapted their mentality of how to think like them quickly so I could get in on another case.

I had two fellow agents that I ran into in and outside the office that were closely working cases like mines; Detective Kyle, who referred to himself as KT in the streets, and undercover Agent Detective Jacobs.

I knew if I wanted to make a name for myself, I would have to create a personality let alone an image for myself such as these guys had already done. I knew this would be easier said than done, so I had already begun meeting with Jacobs and learning the ropes in the field.

Chapter 12

Keys To The City

"Time has come, we got to expand the whole operation, distribution.... We got to set our own mark, and enforce it. We got to think big now."   Al Pacino—Scarface

Barry

"*IN THIS COUNTRY, you got to make the money first, then when you get the money—you get the power, then when you get the power—you get the woman. That's why you got to make your own moves.*"

As time passed, so the level of heist we did. From scores as small as cargo trucks, to out of town bank vaults under heavy surveillance. I made everything so simple and *foolproof* that the heist we took down seemed easy. I had hustlers and goons that wanted to be down with our crew and were just waiting for the right time to prove themselves.

I raised the stakes muscling public and private contracts. Once we acquired the contracts, we usually auctioned them off to the highest bidder. What we were doing already was only the tip of the iceberg. Uncle Billy later put onto big rigging and vote buying.

Those two turned out to be an even bigger payoff when it came to getting police investigations dismissed. Uncle Billy even had *dirt* on crooked judges who we threatened to blackmail if they didn't cooperate.

I made Donell the underboss for my crew. Simply because he was known by every hustler in Dallas plus everyone wanted to be under him.

After being around Donell more and watching him make the transition from the basketball court to the streets, I believed that sometimes he was doing certain things just so he would be taken as a serious drug dealer. He just literally over reacted to situations as if he had something to prove.

Ronnie

Today was the day I had been waiting for after forty-nine months, three weeks and four days- the *free world*.

Walking down my tier for the last time, I knew from here on out, I was going to be there for my brothers so they wouldn't end up in here, or worse in a morgue.

As I walked out the Beaumont Correctional Facility, Barry stood alone dressed sharp as a tack wearing jewelry that confirmed all the rumors I had heard up until now.

"Nigga I know you weren't thinking I got too big to come and get you myself," Barry said with a smile from ear to ear on his face as we embraced each other with open arms.

"Aww man shit, I figured I would have seen you later on tonight, you know with you being a big shot calling Boss and all."

"Aww dawg, I ain't never too big to come and see my mothafuckin' brotha okay."

"Okay, I feel ya. No doubt," I said as we started walking toward the empty convertible Chevrolet Corvette.

"Oh yeah, this is how you doing it now bro?"

Leaning his head back with his arm on my shoulder, he said-

"Naw, this is how *you're* doing it now bro."

"Oh yeah, you're saying this is mines? After being on lockdown for four years, I can ride in this here?"

"You're family and we look out for one another dawg."

"Now hop in the driver seat and take me back to the Westin so we can get ready for a get together tonight."

"Alright then Mr. Jefferson sir, whatever you say Mr. Jefferson sir."

Barry

"You got to be ten toes down and serious about making a mark for yourself out here."

I remembered Uncle Billy telling me as we took our last exit and drove down the service road at Carlos Ranch in Laredo,Tx.

"Man this has got to be the biggest ranch I ever seen bro."

Donell said while driving and staring at the spacious real estate. It was a few miles from the exit and behind the tall trees in front of the driveway, it was very hard to see exactly what was taking place on the porch.

"Man it looks like them dudes got guns in their hands."

Ronnie said leaning toward the dashboard to make out how many people he could count.

"This Mexican is connected bro; he's protected like a motherfucka too."

"All them dudes carrying .223's assault rifles B, you sure these dudes know it's us who pulling up?"

"Yea, they just being careful you know. They may be in some sort of beef with someone else." I said trying to calm their nerves and make sense out the whole situation.

As the Hispanic gunmen approached our Navigator, only one of them began to speak to us, as he himself had a strong accent.

"Ca Cum on homes. Ya'll drive slow enough to do a drive bye *es-say*," the Hispanic dude said while the others who looked on grinned at the joke he was making. I could tell that he was from Los Angeles from the tattoo he had on his neck that read *L.A* in Old English lettering.

As we all got out and scouted our surrounding, we realized it was a very lavish yet elegant built brick home.

"I'm Felix, which one of you is Barry?"

"That's me."

"Come on inside and follow me, my Uncle is waiting for ya'll out back."

Carlos home had columns throughout the house, crystal chandeliers and marble floors as far as my eyes could see. The house was decorated with candles and religious painting of Mary Magdalene and Jesus. As we made it closer to the back patio, we seen his indoor pool, movie theatre and an all glass indoor elevator.

"Amigos, we finally meet again."

Carlos said walking from his backyard as he greeted us with a smile of familiarity.

"I haven't seen you three since you all were lil youngsters."

"Barry me and your father go *waayy*, way back."

"He had my back through a lot of shit when we were in the service. He's a good man, a real friend."

As Carlos escorted us through his lavish estate, we ended up in his game room. Even in his game room, he had an actual arcade, pool tables, and a glassed in recording studio in the back of the room. "Amigo, your pops and I were a tight crew."

"In this business, it's loyalty before royalty and with that being said, that's why I'm sitting here now with you guys."

"Well we're definitely ready to make something happen on a larger scale."

"In case you haven't already heard, I'm the underboss for the Gulf Cartel."

"I can get you all the coke you can dream of amigo, but the number one thing to remember is that you didn't get it from me."

As his mobile phone rung, he slowly stood up.

"Walk with me fellas."

Following him to his yard, I seen he had an outdoor pool house, a stable with horses, and an English Mastiff's kennel. It was then when I noticed a huge hole in the ground. The hole appeared to be dug by a bulldozer as it was neatly trimmed and cornered off at the edges. And it was as if you could walk in and out of it, as it became leveled the more you walked upward. We stood a great distance from it as Carlos stopped while on the phone looking at the huge square shaped hole. Then that's when I heard Felix voice echoing from it-

"Aqurate."

"Estate en linea."

"Casi estas alli."

As Felix walked out of what was actually a tunnel, Felix turned with his back to us facing the tunnel, while at the same time walking backwards, instructing the group of people using the length of a double barrel shotgun to point with.

"Dejalos," he said while pointing at the empty moving boxes that were sat aside by a U-HAUL truck.

"Wow Carlos man what the hell is that?" Donell said in shock as he couldn't believe what was taking place.

As Felix instructed the horde of dirty, dusty and exhausted Hispanic immigrants to empty their hands, he led them around the side of the house.

Carlos was downright smuggling illegal immigrants into the states through an underground tunnel in his backyard. He even had each of the people carrying saran wrapped bundles of already packaged cocaine.

"Each one carries five kilo's amigo."

Carlos said observing and giving orders through his hand held radio to workers carrying machine guns who had not yet emerged from the tunnel.

As we all got back into Donell's SUV, we just sat there and stared at the massive estate and thought of everything we just seen taking place. I wondered if our pops knew about this.

I sat in the backseat uncertain of whether or not we were getting ourselves in too deep. I realized now that there were different sides to this game and that there are something's that I just didn't want to know or be apart of.

As the SUV shook a little bit while the Mexican men hooked the U-Haul truck onto our Navigator, I couldn't help but do the math in my head.

Fifty people each carrying five kilo's, half of which was on consignment and the other half of which we paid for at four grand a kilo. We may have been putting up half a million dollars, but by selling them at thirteen thousand-five hundred a kilo, we would almost triple our profit at two point eight million dollars.

"Just do the speed limit, all we go to do is make it back." I told Donell as calmly as I could

Chapter 13

Keep A Strong Arm

". . . I ain't a killer but don't push me—Revenge is like the sweetest joy next to getting pussy. . . If it's on then it's on, we break beat-breaks. ."
Hail Mary—Tupac ft. Outlaws

"YOU YOUNG MOTHAFUCKA .... If you don't get the fuck off my property, I'll smoke yo ass before my man right here finishes his cigarette."

Big John said cockily standing outside the back of his popular nightclub *VIP*.

"Ya'll niggas rob trains, and bully squares. Who the fuck are ya'll to come and make me a deal?"

"Oh okay, I see how you want to play the game nigga."

Trey said heatedly walking to his Audi A8. Trey was a friend of Donell's, but was the second in charge when it came to pulling off heist. Trey was only acting on behalf of Barry in terms of negotiating a price to deal cocaine for wholesale only to Big John.

"Nigga we ain't fucking playing!" Big John yelled out gesturing toward his gunmen that stood beside him.

"Ya'll niggas ain't shit but the next *Jessie James* crew!"

"Nigga you got the whole game fucked up if you think we're not going to put it down in this city!"

Trey shouted out the driver side window slowly pulling out the parking lot.

I'ma show them niggas tha meaning of respect.

Big John thought as he instructed his enforcers to tail Trey car from a distance, and once he was far enough from the club to make him out as an example.

Barry

I was making so much money that my competition couldn't keep up. Every visit with Carlos was more like hitting a power ball.

With the way Big John treated the younger hustlers, the timing couldn't have been better for my crew to put our foot down in the game. It was almost like déjà vu during my senior years in college when it came to all the drugs and duffle bags of money we made.

At every peak, you still have your lows.

I would often think when it came to how my operations were taking off faster than expected. I was keeping less and less *tabs* of how Des and Jr ran their operation, which proved to be fatal in return. Almost on a weekly basis, I was getting phone calls from dealers in different states about how Des was knocking hustlers off because they didn't want to share their turf. As if that wasn't already enough, I was getting collect calls just as much from dealers that knew they were under investigation because of how Jr. was splurging his money and making it obvious as to what he—and everyone he associated with did for a living. I was confused as to how two brothers could both be making plenty of money, yet still working against one another.

This is Christie Wetworth with Fox 4 bringing you breaking news on the drive by homicide case here in the City of Dallas. It hasn't even been one hour since this shooting took place and as you can see behind me—there is already a crowd of spectators gathering around the scene.

Leaning forward out of my chair, I looked on at the flat screen monitor, when I thought I recognized the car but wasn't sure just yet.

Police and forensic detectives have just identified the victim in this dreadful accident by the name of Trey Johnson. The ambulance and paramedic pronounced Trey Johnson, who is actually only twenty-four years old, DOA when they responded. Some of you may remember this gentleman as one of the few young men who was apprehended by the police for drug possession about a year and a half ago along with statewide leading basketball scorer Donell McCoy.

"Aww hell naw!"

As the news camera took different shots of Trey's car being riddled with bullet holes, it seemed surreal by the number of bullets that were spilled into the doors and windows. Not only did the car have bullets holes in it from the trunk to the hood, but also the tires were even shot out.

That nigga never stood a chance.

All I could think of was how Trey was always trying to step up in the game. He was always so damn *hungry* . . . A real go getta. When I seen him struggling I took him into my crew—in which he got into head first, and now look at him, all because of me.

Donell

Damn . . . I was just on the phone with him. He shouldn't have gone out like that.

As I was greeted at the door by one of Barry's girlfriends, my long-term girlfriend Rhonda followed me into his posh Victorian styled home.

Barry was completely engaged in his conversation as he only acknowledged me with a head nod and continued on listening.

"That mothafucka got some fucking nerves! That could have been me in that damn car! I tried coming correct and niggas want to disrespect! That mothafucka done fucked up . . . He just so happen to luck up by not killing me first Des!"

Aww shit. As if matters couldn't get any worse, he just had to be on the phone with someone who could. Those two brothers earned the nicknamed Tha Killa Duo and lived up to all the hype that came with it.

I knew things were going to get turned up a notch when I heard Des name.

"Yea..Yea. Nigga ya'll just need to get ya'll asses to *Plan B* quicker than shit."

Talking into two phones simultaneously, this was the most upset I'd ever seen him as he now stared into my direction.

"You . . . You get your shit and get ready to head out."

Barry said with a nonsense look on his face. He had spoken to me as if I already knew what he wanted, let alone what he was talking about. By my side, Rhonda stood looking as puzzled as I was when she began to point at herself.

"Barry are you talking to me?"

She said innocently not wanting to interrupt Barry listening on the phone.

"Barry baby . . . His sister just called and said she's at the police station waiting on us to come and get her."

The exotic looking girl that answered the door said while twirling the phone in a nonchalant fashion.

"Hell yeah, I'm talking to you . . . I want you to go and head down to the police station and get Trey sister before child protective services start snooping around."

Being that Rhonda usually did Trey's sister hair, they had somewhat of a connection as she didn't argue back with Barry. Regardless of me being her ride, finding a car to drive wouldn't be hard at all being that Barry had a convoy of Beamer's, Benz's and Bentley's in his driveway.

Leaving the house, Barry speedily swerved his S550 Benz as if he was Dale Earnhardt when we pulled up into JD's driveway in record timing.

"Is everybody here?"

Barry said quickly as he exited the car a little sooner than I did.

As Barry and I were escorted by JD, the neon lights surrounding the pool lit the backyard up as the wooden fences were covered with hustlers and enforcers from everywhere. They gave Ronnie their undivided attention.

"I'm going to let ya'll niggas now, that if you ain't riding with us, then you're against us."

"I want that nigga whole fucking crew swept off the streets—from his runners to his right hand man. I don't give a flying fuck!" Ronnie said standing in the center of Barry and me. Barry reminded me of our pops the way he lit his cigar and looked around before speaking.

"Look . . . . Ya'll know why we're here. You know who we're going after; regardless of who did what before us . . . I'll plug all ya'll into game myself."

When the meeting was over, dealers slowly left talking among themselves as to how Big John held out on supplying them with drugs and now they knew they were all going to be able to make some money with Barry calling the shots in town.

The next week and a half that went by was nothing short of the *Wild Wild West*. If I wasn't driving down a street that was blocked off with yellow caution tape around it, I was watching the forensic Investigators draw chalk around a dead body.

Every since that night, henchmen wasted no time going after Big John and his crew. From the runners all the way up to his Captains—the same man that was once a feared as an *Original Gangster* was now a target in his hometown.

"Shit Donell . . . We're riding with you and your brother on this one cause Barry done had our back every since he came back home."

From the neighborhood carwash to the barbershops, the players in Big John circle were nowhere to be found. The turning point was when hustlers found out that Ronnie was out of prison. Ronnie surprised everyone showing up at JD's house that night. It wasn't long after that night that Ronnie reminded everyone who he was when he walked up and shot Big John brother in the head in broad daylight outside of his own house. Big John then went into hiding after his brother was murdered which was when Barry began to grow more and more impatient .

"Yo man . . . Is it true that your brother put a fifty-thousand dollar bounty on Big John head?"

"Shid you know how the game goes . . . When it rains, niggas get wet."

I said with my head down getting my haircut. It was then when I received a beep from a number that appeared to be Ronnie followed by *911*.

Once I called Ronnie back and met up with him, we rode together while he filled in me on the latest news.

"Yo D . . . What happened was I ended up getting a phone call from a friend of mines I met a while back in the joint."

He said as we rode toward the outskirts of the city on a dirt path service road alongside the freeway.

"John has been out here at his stash house every since *B* put that money on his head."

"Oh yeah . . . Damn this dude been out here for a while then."

"Yeah he has . . . But like I told Barry when we were younger. Any dude that starts beef with one of ya'll is going to have a problem with me too."

After driving through the wooded area, we finally arrived at the stash house where John was hiding. I could tell that he hadn't spent much time outside neither, as the lawn hadn't been cut in weeks. With a birds eye view of his entire property, we just sat there waiting in the car.

Every since Ronnie had came home, I could tell he had changed, not just physically but mentally. It was as though he had a strong urge to protect Barry and myself since he had gotten out.

"See, there he is now . . . Leaving out, locking his burglar bar doors."

Ronnie said nodding forward as we both scrunched our eyes watching John walk down his steps. Ronnie then pointed at a guy that was on the roof with a sniper rifle watching everything take place.

BAP BAP PING!!!

The noises caught my attention to look back at John as I could see that he was being beaten with wood and metal bats by dudes with ski mask on.

"AHHH!!! OUCH! AHHH!"

The men used Johns' ribs, knees and arms as batting practice as they took turns viciously beating him. Ronnie then rolled down the driver side window.

"Not tha face! Don't touch his face!"

Ronnie and I then got out and gradually walked down the dirt path, observing the men tape John hands and feet before pulling the sock off his own foot and stuffing it into his mouth. Joined by the man that was once on the roof, Ronnie acknowledged him.

"This dude right here is my nigga . . . . We met while I was locked up, this is Bodie."

"Wassup D.. I read a lot about you while in the joint about you playing ball and all."

"Yeah . . . Yeah, that's what's up."

"Yeah Ronnie, this nigga paid me ten grand to watch his house. It wasn't until I was at a gas station when I overheard some dudes talking about how your brother Barry put a bounty of fifty grand on the same nigga head."

He said as he positioned the shoulder strap of the riffle across his chest watching the masked men put John into the trunk of his own car. As JD and Cap took of their mask, we all shook hands as they made fun of the faces John was making when they were beating him.

Up until the time when Ronnie and I finally got around to telling Barry that we had Big John, hustlers already assumed that Big John ran out of town. Nowadays, when I would be shopping at the mall, or out clubbing, the street hustlers in the city no longer looked at me as *Mr. Basketball* of Dallas.

"Bro, we're making so much money nowadays it's scary."

I said to Barry while driving to a cemetery to meet up with Ronnie and Benny.

"This is what we're in this for. I'm going to turn our little crew into a fortune 500 underground empire."

"I can dig that."

I said in agreement because up until Barry had come home, I didn't think I would see the chance of making it out the hood and becoming someone famous. Now that we making more and more money, I knew it was possible. I had saved and put away over half a million dollars and had no intensions of slowing down.

I'm going to be a motherfuckin' professional gangster.

The way Barry, Ronnie and I ran the city, it felt like the *The American Dream*. "Yo man, is that punk ass nigga still alive?"

I said to Benny while walking over to the trunk of Johns' car.

"Yeah he is. He finally stopped kicking and screaming and shit."

Although it was 5:30 a.m., I could tell that John had not gotten any sleep by the look in his eyes.

"Now tell me . . . How you want mothafuckas' to find your body?"

"In one of these empty graves, floating in a river or shot up with bullet holes like Trey?"

Barry said while standing over him blowing weed smoke in his face.

"See . . . Nigga, I told yo ass that you don't know who you're fucking with."

"Remove the sock from this nigga mouth so he can talk will you Benny?"

"C'mon man Barry . . . Ya'll know how the game go."

"Some young niggas come up on the scene out of nowhere and try to run shit . . . You would have tried to defend what's yours too."

John said staring into Barry's eyes with a look of desperation.

"Well . . . These streets ain't yours no more- they're mines."

"Now, how much money you got . . . You can buy yo life back John."

As Ronnie and I looked from John to Barry with a look of confusion on our faces, I could only imagine.

Don't this nigga know that if we let him live, he's definitely going to come back for our ass.

"Yeah . . . Yeah, I can do that baby boy. I got four hundred thousand."

"It's in a safe that I got in a house over on North West Hwy. Seven-teen, thirty-four, twenty-eight."

Just as soon as John stutteringly finished his sentence, Barry nonchalantly shook his head from side to side.

"Uhmp uhmp uhmp . . .That's not enough anymore. We'll be sure to make show that Trey little sister gets some of that money though."

"Wha . . . What?""

"You no good motherfucka! Who the hell you think you are? You better let me out this motherfucka!" John said as he screamed and shouted. While Barry and I walked back to my Ferrai 360 Spider, we opened the doors as we watched Ronnie pour gasoline into the trunk and all over John as he shouted profanity at him and Benny.

Benny then got into the passenger side and slowly drove off while at the same time leaving behind a trail of gasoline lighter fluid from the car to the main street. Ronnie then walked over to the end of the trail and put his blunt out into the gasoline. Right at that moment, the trail of gasoline turned into a blazing line of fire all the way back to the trunk that John was tied up in causing John to burn up alive just before the car exploded.

"Ashes to ashes and dust to dust mothafucker."

I said out the window while Barry and I drove to pick up some drugs from Felix on the other side of town.

Chapter 14

All For the Taking

"... For real G, I'ma fullfill my dream
If I conceal my scheme, then precisely I'll build my cream.."
NAS-Street Dreams

"... I'm not going to end up like he did all right.."
Tyrin "Caine" Turner—Menace to Society (Film)

Barry

NOWADAYS, I FELT like Butch Johnson when he ran the YBI. With Kingston and Blue supplying my crew on the east coast and Carlos being my connection back home- I was unstoppable.

With all the law enforcement agencies trying to keep tabs on my brother and I, I soon realized that once you reach the top, life was nothing but a game.

I made sure I stayed two steps ahead of the cops. I knew that they were on my trail because no matter what state, in every city I went to, it was as if I never left home. Every hustler knew me and my brother. Whether I was shopping on Rodeo Drive in California or dining at Lawry's in Chicago, woman flocked on our coattail.

I put my money into legitimate dealings. I opened up day cares, gun shops and nightclubs. It went without saying to those who actually *knew* me, knew that they were all a front to drop off and pick up either drugs or guns or both.

Donell loved every bit of the *American Dream*. He would refer to himself as an *American Gangster. It was as if he was a* third person with an alter ego.

"I hear what you're saying... But the gangster in me just can't wait until the nigga plays his hand, I got to make sure his ass gets dealt with."

The streets were talking, and Donell was making his presence felt with all the lavish sports cars, high priced bets and large amounts of money he surrounded himself with.

While Donell pursued the *American Dream*, I applied pressure to business owners. I had my own extortion and racketeering operations that were bringing down numbers just as easy as the drug money.

With the local cops on our tail, we completely stopped taking scores from trains, and banks because the cash flow from the drug money came off too smoothly. Besides, I had my own Cartel connection and was able to supply all the dealers that Des and Jr. once did.

Some dealers were repeated buyers like one named Wayne. Wayne was trying to make a name for himself by dealing large amounts of heroin. Before Donell dealt with him, he had Stanley check him out. Everyone had to get checked out these days because the FED's were trying to infiltrate us more and more.

The more I paid the Police Commissioner, the State Troopers and a few undercover confidential informants- the more they all said the same thing. The ATF, DEA, FBI and U.S. Marshalls are all coming after my entire crew. I received the majority of my information from an undercover agent known in the streets as KT.

I could recall a dozen reasons as to why the FED's would have my crew under surveillance. From all the murders that I gave the okay for to the amount of guns we sold, which in return we used to make business owners pay up. Hell, I could even go as far back as to all the stolen retail merchandise we sold off the trains we robbed. Not to mention the city councilmen we exploited, bribed and threaten to blackmail.

Looking outside my window, the caged bob wired fence was a undeniable reminder of how much I hated the prison system.

Federal Correctional Institution Bastrop

"Sir, remove all metal items and turn off your cell phone."

While I waited in the room for visitors, I felt as though I was tempted to buy my pops some chips or soda but then I thought back to the reason why I never had bought anything for him up until now.

"If you ever have to do something for me, it's going to be making my funeral arrangements because Dave Leroy McCoy will never want for shit."

My pops never sent me any money orders to put money on his books after all this time and he even told my mom, to tell me not to send him nothing but put it back for myself.

I spotted him behind the glass wearing a tan creased jump suite. Pops was the only dude in line who had a gold link bracelet, a gold pinky ring and some timberland boots. Approaching me slowly, I could tell he had put on a good twenty pounds of pure muscle when I noticed the grey hairs growing in his goatee.

"How you been son?"

"I've been doing well. You know, same ole shit just a different day."

The moment I finished my sentence, my pops looked over his shoulder before removing his prison ID badge when he turned his attention back to me. Withdrawing a gold link Mavodo watch from his pants pocket and placing it around his wrist, I noticed that it had a diamond where the twelfth hour was.

"Damn CO's be stealing," he said under his breath before looking to me.

"Larry Hover got caught up with the bugs they put on these badges."

He said as he headed toward the vending machine behind me to place it on the ground and buy a bag of chips.

"Now let's try this again. How have you been?"

"I been busy . . . I been putting together a little crew and whatnot—you know, making moves that make moves," I said halfway disappointed that my pops was three years into a life sentence, and this was the first time I was visiting him.

"Well . . . Although that isn't the life I'd rather you choose, I hope you're thinking ahead and intend on getting out soon."

"You see... the only thing you're seeing right now is what looks good for you, but what you don't see is what's best for you."

"Like you're doing now, I was doing the same when I was out there. I got so caught up in the moves that I was making, that I started putting the thoughts I should have made first last."

The tone in pops voice was starting to hit home. He always had that way about him- getting his point across the first time. I guess that's why our mother always would tell our pops to talk to my brother and me when we would get in trouble. Dad didn't have to whip us coming up, hell we wanted to be like him.

"I never told you and your brother about what I did on the side because I didn't want ya'll to confuse what you choose to do on the side with what you shouldn't do at all."

"I hear you and I am, but I can handle my own. How bout yourself?"

"Shit... You know I can."

"I can get what I want when I want it; I been a *made man* long before I got here."

"You know . . . You and your brother could have been anything ya'll wanted to be. But what you have to remember is that, it's not how much wrong you do, but how long you decide to keep doing wrong."

"Mothfuckas talk about you guys like ya'll the Mob, as if ya'll some type of underground Syndicate,"

"Is that what ya'll call yourselves?"

"No . . . Naw pops, I just got a lot of soldiers."

Pops shook his head before slightly grinning at me.

"You think you got it all figured, but ya'll don't even know what the word on the street is."

As we talked some more about the ends and outs of the game, we later went on to talk about family matters such as how my brother was making a lot of money but didn't have any street credibility—which in return would have to be earned sooner or later. Pops and I talked all the way up until visiting hours were over. As I was leaving, my pops slowly rose to hug me.

"I would rather you have chose to play football but you're your own man. And with that being said, I want you to always remember one thing."

"The most important decision you have to make now is keeping track of your timing. Your timing has everything to do with whether or not you will end up in here where I' am. Just like you feel as though the timing couldn't have been better to come into the game, you can rest assure that the same feeling will come around one more last time. Only this time you will feel as though it's time to get out."

The talk I had with my pops made me think. I thought that maybe I should get out now while I was being warned and get Donell in contact with some college recruiters. Although I was being warned of my future, I was living life right now, and if I was suppose to get a feeling telling me to get out, I definitely didn't have it now.

Detective Johnson

All my hard work had finally paid off. Not only did I meet players making moves, but granted to pursue independently an already up and upcoming midlevel organization.

Based on the information I had so far, the crew that composed of three brothers were engaged in; cargo heist, gun running, contract killing, extortion, drug trafficking as well as money laundering and fencing. I soon found out that these men were more than average but unexpectedly sharp. Jaz, Det. Jacobs had brought me up to speed as far as creating a new identity to be perceived as, which allowed me to initially infiltrate the outer circle of their close curriors such as Stanley and Baby Blue.

"*You have to be bold. You can't fear nothing or no man. You got to act like you live this life, as if this is all you actually know.*"

I remember Det. Jacobs telling me one day as we went and checked out some

seized weapons that I was to sell.

Over this period, I had gotten to know Det. Jacobs very well, both professionally and personally. He taught me about how to be a better undercover detective. Detective Jacobs was a family man with a wife and two sons that he kept pictures of at the office as well as his wedding ring.

It just so happen to be that today Jacobs was taking me along for the ride as we were going to make our second to last large sale of machine guns. The dude he had been dealing with trusted him a lot and didn't question him when he said he was bringing a friend.

"*Yeah he believes in me Johnson, and that's the same impression you need to give off. You got to blend in by any means necessary Johnson. Because if you don't, they're going to make and take you out.*"

Det. Jacobs told me while we were on our way to meet up with a fella named Short Dogg from New York. He had been buying at least ten grand worth of weapons every other week. He even went as far as to asking for grenades and grenade launchers.

"*Yeah, I'm going to play these motherfucka alright; I'm going to play them to the T.*"

I said aloud as I patted down my Teflon vest.

Chapter 15

The Commission

"... . Gotta take the good with the bad, smile with the sad, love what you got and remember what you had ..."
Project Pat—Life We Live

Barry

AS THE SUMMER of '98 came to an end, so did the gossip of how notorious and strong in numbers my crew had become. It got to the point where I decided to address it to Donell and Ronnie while over at Ronnie's condo.

"Yo man, I got a name for us and everyone in our crew, from our soldiers to the boss's... We should call ourselves a Mafia. Hell we're already making moves like a mafia."

"Mafia... Let me see, you got the Italian mafia, the Russian mafia... What you're going to name ours?"

Ronnie said holding a cup of Hypnotic and Hennessy, with his back leaning up against the bar counter top.

"The Money Mobb Mafia. We're going to spell Mob with two B's though. They will stand for Black Brothers, you feel me?"

"Damn man, that shit sounds heavy. That shit sounds gangster. I like it."

Donell said while staring off into what seemed like space.

"Money Mobb Mafia huh? Well we're damn show making money."

Donell added leaning back playing with his diamond necklace charm. It was obvious how Donell spent his money on jewelry, cars and custom tailored clothes.

"What you think Ronnie?"

"I think that's not something we should do to be honest with you."

"I think it's an easier way for the police to associate us with one another.

I mean, if we take on the name Mafia, the same politicians and crooked police officers are going to stray away from being affiliated with us."

"So you're not feeling the name, is that what you trying to say?"

"Look B, I'm down with you two through whatever. We're a team and the way I see it, we're too close to having the American Dream to slow down now bro."

"Okay then . . . We'll put the word out that it's us against the world. Money Mobb Mafia over everything… We're underground kings."

Toasting our glasses, we already dressed and had all the material things that proved we were living life at its best, but I had dreams on becoming even bigger.

Special Agent Logan & Det. Johnson

It seemed as though my entire world centered on this case. Barry, Donell and Ronnie McCoy were big time dealers that had an excess of artillery as well. Through Stanley, Donell's best friend, I was able to buy large quantities of cocaine from them as well as extra amounts, on consignment.

Not only was I driving their drugs across the country, but I was also transporting money on behalf of his colleagues Des and Jr that headed up the operations in North Carolina. Des and Jr were always in the spotlight; from shootouts to clubbing unlike Barry who was always quiet and inconspicuous.

"How we're looking? Are you ready to take this dude down Johnson?"

Logan asked me standing in his civilian attire planning to visit the field arrest and witness us taking down Short Dogg.

"Oh yeah, more than ever, I was born for this, Sir."

"Okay, well I'll be watching, Detective."

This dude Barry McCoy was smarter than smart, but downright ingenious when it came to how he would put distance in-between any acts being committed. Now his brother Donell on the other hand, was getting more and more big headed and known throughout the city of his illegal ties. With the help of wire taped audio conversations, the Bureau had all we needed to take down Short Dogg for a contract killing on behalf of Donell.

"Ladies and gentlemen, this is a crime scene and you are to stand at a safe distance from what has taken place." I observed the uniformed officer saying as I went back and forward from the house to my car.

During the raid, I sat behind the tinted windows in the squad car and witnessed two local police officers get killed and three ATF agents get injured. Det. Jacobs was practically unharmed since he was three times the size of Short Dogg, tackling him before cuffing him. It was his crew that retaliated shooting everyone else in the process.

"Johnson, I want you to go inside and collect the guns that we found hidden in their bedrooms." Jacobs said as the squad car drove off with Short Dogg in the back.

Ronnie

When we labeled our crew the Money Mobb Mafia, business started *booming* the way every hustler wanted to score drugs, guns and be down with us. Our name rang bells from city to city.

As far as the neighborhood went, Barry decided to start and coach a little league football team. Within the first year of his coaching, they won their first little league championship.

Donell on the other hand, immediately began coaching a basketball team for teenagers, in which they went all the way to the city finals. Despite their lost, Donell was so happy that he took all the team players shopping with him a few days later.

I, myself was more so into throwing block parties with paid for clowns, air castles, food and cash prize giveaways. I made a popular locally resigned police sergeant head up my community organization from which Barry and Donell's teams originated.

As I rolled by Short Dogg house, I was taken aback by the amount of squad cars that surrounded his house. There were the ATF, DEA and U.S. Marshall Agents wearing their Bureau jackets everywhere. The house was in shambles with bullet holes riddled throughout the walls as the windows were shot out as well.

"*This is some crazy ass shit.*"

Observing the agents wearing their windbreaker jackets, one particularly stood out. His hoody and sunglasses covered up his face. He was the only man in street clothes, until another man in street clothes wearing a badge emerged from the house giving him instructions on what to do next.

I definitely stored the image of the man giving the orders wearing street clothes into the back of my mind, as I perceived him to be an undercover agent. However, it was the face of his counterpart that I wish I could have seen.

Chapter 16

Respect It or Check It

"..I'm going to kill your mother, your two kids, and that fat ugly bitch of your's... Then I'm going to come looking for you and I'ma blow your heart out your body sucker."   *Max Julien—The Mack(Film)*

Donell

JUST AS FAST as we scored the drugs, the faster every player *out of the woodworks* wanted to buy them. We were supplying hustlers from as far as Nevada to Roxbury Projects in Boston. I was starting to feel the pressure the more we had to go and *re-up* for drugs from Felix if not Carlos.

I, myself was moving so much cocaine that in some instances, I would use Stanley to do drop off's and deliveries. The problem with using Stanley was that he didn't tell the mid-level players he dealt with that he was down with the Money Mobb Mafia. I believed that was why sometimes he would have troubles collecting the monies that were owed to him. When I would get to the bottom of the issues, I learned that most of the time it was hustlers who he fronted drugs on consignment to that owed him.

As the State Fair of Texas came, so did all the big spenders in the city. The State Fair brought women from all over. And I knew Ronnie hadn't ever been before and I wanted him to go with me.

"Look man, you're going to the Grambling vs. Prairie View game with me, this shit isn't an option."

"Nigga who in the hell died and left you in charge."

"Look bro, just roll with me to a few places and then to the game later on, at least watch my back."

"Uhmm, I guess man. I'm going to go ahead and roll with you because you're turning into a high profile player now."

Ronnie

I don't know why this dude has me in this store, but I wasn't really feeling all the shopping and whatnot. Donell had me thinking that I was going to be watching his back, but instead we had been everywhere spending money and not picking anything up.

From Neiman Marcus to the jewelry store, I didn't know why he insisted on dressing me up like some sort of *pretty boy*. I mean I never understood why Donell always wanted to be referred to as the fly and flashiest player.

After spending ten grand on me on a Gucci outfit, he insisted that I leave out the store wearing it. He then went on to his jeweler and bought me a Presidential Rose gold Rolex flooded with diamonds.

"Man…. This shit is too fucking much."

"Ronnie you can't be thuggin' all the time bro. You got to relax man, you're too uptight."

That was easy to say from the outside, but on the inside I was all messed up. The voices I began hearing in prison had gotten worse now. My reflexes we all jittery, I was on edge all the time. When Donell and Barry was VIP everywhere they went, I felt alone. What went on in my mind, and what I had been through in life kept me up late at nights. I sometimes thought of seeing a shrink or therapist as someone with whom to talk. I mean I didn't want my brothers thinking I was losing my mind or anything. However, at the same time, I knew I was starting to get overwhelmed with the things I was going through. Exiting the store, I got into the driver side and Donell got in on the passenger side when he just starred at me.

"Now you're an official fly *mu-tha-fucka!*" He said displaying a super sized smile on his face.

Barry

"Wassup bro?"

"Shit, nigga you know the rules, I should hang up the phone right motherfucking now," I said irritated that Short Dogg had called me direct from the county jail.

"Chill G, I got some real shit hot off the press that can take us both out the game."

"Shit go head then."

After making out what Short was saying in-between his New York accent, I was glad that I had taken the phone call. What had appeared to everybody as a supposedly ATF raid was actually a set up between himself and an undercover federal agent who was still out there and possibly pursing the Mobb.

Damn, I need to get this motherfucka name so we can pull the plug on this rat. Short Dogg wanted the Mobb to kill the Agent so he wouldn't be able to testify against him, and I on the other hand wanted him dead so he wouldn't be able to testify against anyone else.

Waiting for the right time to use my ace in the hole, I began to call up an undercover agent that Billy introduced me to whom I had been paying off on the down low. So far he'd been useful up until now as far as keeping us two steps ahead of the FED's, but know he was definitely going to earn his pay.

Donell

While riding to the Grambling and Prairie View game, I meditated on how I overseen the drug, fencing and arms trafficking side of the Mobb business, while Barry would handle more of the extortion and racket side. From what I had seen, the money from extorting business owners and blackmailing politicians was just as easy.

When I looked over at my cousin, I knew it was more than the clothes I bought him that made him uncomfortable. I knew it was still something bothering him in the back of his mind, but I couldn't quite lay my finger on it, so I figured that was just because he wasn't used to really looking like new money.

Checking my beeper, I got heated just that fast when I seen Stanley texting me the code *211*, meaning some hustlers didn't pay him. *I'm going after those motherfuckas myself.*

Just like the Italian and the Philadelphia Mafia had rules, so did we damit!

You pay your debts, and you pay who you owe! Whether it's street taxes or whatever, the rules don't favor, bend or break for nobody.

Slim, Rich and Jerry were officially on my *knock'em off list*. Stanley ran down to me their M.O. while Ronnie and I were in the jewelry store, and I could tell from the sound of it that they would definitely be at the game later on. Well, to their surprise I would be there too, with the baddest mothafucka in the city with me.

Ronnie

Pulling up into the parking lot at the State Fair, I was overwhelmed by the crowd as we rode the train to the entrance.

I stood beside Donell as he went about shaking hands, and introducing me to everybody. He knew hustlers from all over. The more I listened to him, it seemed as though nine times out of ten, they got their drugs from the Mobb.

"See, that's D.J, he's from the Southside of Houston, they wear red."

While making our way through the crowd, I watched Donell step to one chick after another. He kept talking to me as if he was schooling me at the same time.

"Listen Ron, you got to just do it bro. Fuck all that thinking shit. A chick like it when you do shit without hesitating."

"Well how do I even know if they like me like that?"

"It's in the eyes bro. The eyes don't lie, trust me."

Donell

As the game went on and ended, everyone went from the Cotton Bowl to inside the State Fair afterwards. It wasn't until we stopped in front of the Ferris wheel, when I seen the *baddest* chick I had ever laid eyes on. She had to be Hispanic by the looks of it. She had long blond hair that shined like satin sheets and the most mesmerizing eyes ever. Her eyebrows were arched, making her look seductive and erotic at the same time. She was slim and fine with a silky vanilla coated skin completion. She couldn't have been any taller than 5'6 at a hundred and thirty pounds. She had a sexy pair of breast to match her petite 36c-26-40 frame, with a fat apple shaped ass to go with her small waistline.

Boldly beginning to make my way toward her, I looked back only to see Ronnie shooting water guns still trying to win our Aunt a teddy bear. Then that's exactly when I seen Slim and Rich standing by looking on as the Latino chick politely turned Jerry down after a few words. Slim immediately recognized me.

"Yo Donell, what's up homie?"

"You know what the fuck is up, where's the money you owe Stanley?"

"Oh yea, man we're going to pay him alright. The hood just been kind of *slow motion* ya feel me." he said as he looking away from me.

"Well now ya'll owe the Mobb, so Ronnie and I come to collect that shit! So give it up mothafucka!"

As Jerry finally joined into the circle in front of me, I saw the Latino chick outside my peripheral vision looking on at the whole thing. For a moment, it seemed as though she was looking past me.

"Aww naw man, you don't have to send Ronnie to collect. Hell, I'll give you everything I got right now." Rich said as he reached into his pocket handing me a wad of crisp one hundred dollar bills.

"That there is two thousand dollars," he said looking at the other two to pay the rest of what was owed while he walked off behind them to the parking lot.

It was when I seen them looking clueless at one another when I pulled out my pistol from my coat pocket.

"I see I'm going to have to check ya'll niggas."

Ronnie

The instant I took the teddy bear from the man behind the counter, I turned around only to hear people yelling.

"Look out! He's got a gun!"

Women scattered screaming.

"This nigga done lost his rabbit ass mind."

I couldn't see the reason why Donell would pull a gun out in the middle of a crowd like this, especially with so many people around. Anybody could have gotten in the way of his shot.

When I headed in Donell's direction, I caught a glimpse of an exotic looking Latino chick. She stood out in the panic filled crowd as if she was the only one, while holding a super sized teddy bear in her arms. Her crème-colored Bebe denim body suit seemed as though it was hand painted on her coke bottle curvy body all the way down to the pair of tan trimmed Manolo Blahnik boots that matched her tan colored wool jacket.

We made brief eye contact for what seemed like a moment too long, causing me to lose sight of where Donell had ran off too.

Once behind the steering wheel of my SUV, I drove up and down the street looking for anything that seemed out of place.

Tired of weaving through all the traffic, I pulled inside the parking lot of a major intersection so he could see my truck. After a second look, I rolled down the passenger side window to make sure I was seeing whom

I thought I was seeing. It was the same Latino chick from inside the fair that was leaving the restaurant. When she looked to where the music was coming from, we made eye contact once again.

"It's in the eyes, bro. The eyes don't lie."

Halfway nervous thinking of what to say, I exited my truck. By time I realized I left my car running, I was already standing in front of her.

"I'm glad to see you again minus the madness." I said scrambling to think of what to say next.

"With the glow in your eyes, those gunshots may have been fireworks the more I think about it." I said when I noticed her smile before blushing.

"Oh yeah... I was wondering why you walked away?" She asked as I watched the words roll right off her sexy lips. Then she added, "I think you're kinda cute. And you're tall to . . . I like that."

As my mind was going blank, I took my hand outside my jacket and reached to shake her's while asking for her name.

"Oh I'm Christina."

After we exchanged numbers, I headed back to my truck with her slightly beside me, all the while looking back before asking me-

"You weren't scared of someone taking your truck?"

"Naw baby girl . . . Anything that's mines is off limits to everyone else. " I said smirking and adding, "Someone jacking me is the least of my worries."

Donell

Tired from walking through the grass field, I was thankful to see Ronnie SUV parked in the parking lot. I saw then that Ronnie was getting that fine ass Latino girl number, and decided not to even interrupt him with what had just happened. I was happy just to see him doing his thing.

Taking a phone call, Ronnie held the phone to his ear silently asking me what the hell happened as I sat there still breathing heavily.

"Nothing... Call the crew and tell them I got a job for'em."

"Turns out that Barry want to meet up with us about a rat in our circle."

"A fucking rat? You got to be shitting me. How in the fuck are we supposed to put a finger on who it could be?

"He says he already knows who it is, and he's going to set it all up for *you to* handle." Ronnie said as if I was calling the shots, which was something I could get used to doing.

Chapter 17

Unfinished Business

"An eye for an eye so now yo life is what you owe me, look deep into the eyes of yo motherfuckin killer I want you to witness yo motherfuckin murder nigga..."   *No Tears—Scarface (Rapper)*

Ronnie

IN BETWEEN ALL the contract murders and kidnappings for ransom, it seemed as though my mind got more and more tangled as my thoughts housed complete pandemonium.

Deep in thought about how fast things were taking off around me, Christina called me about the whereabouts concerning my mother whom I haven't heard from in I don't know how long.

From when we initially met to when my mother had gone missing, Christina and I had grown to learn quite a bit about one another. It felt like perfect timing by the way in which we had met in the midst of everything. She had an aura about herself that was relaxing, yet when she spoke she sounded so understanding. She was interested in my past and how I had become so mentally strong. Our bond grew closer the more I became myself around here and took the advice she offered in terms of how the nightmares might have meaning behind them.

When Aunt Juanita escorted me around her new condominium, I immediately took a liking to how it was decorated. Her place was filled with pictures of Donell, Barry and I all over the living room and throughout the hallway.

"I'm going to get straight to it because I love you and I want you to know the truth." She said sitting behind her kitchen table drinking tea.

"Ronnie baby, your mother, my sister Deborah has been gone quite some time and last night they found her." She said as I watched the tears silently fall down her face.

"Now Ronnie baby, your mom was an addict indeed, but she wasn't always like that. It wasn't until she met a man that wanted to be with her more than she wanted to be with him. You see baby... Your mother was very much engaged in college at SMU and making very good grades."

"She was also in a complicated relationship with the man that wanted to be with her. She tried to distance herself from him because he was a drug dealer that used drugs himself, but he was abusive too."

"She ended getting pregnant with you by him, and even though she planned to go back to school, she got involved in drugs and he left her."

"He left her after she became hooked on the drugs he turned her onto." She said putting emphasis on her last words.

"He's been around your mother visiting more and more. His name is Eddie and everybody in the neighborhood refers to him as-

"Eddie B."

"Yea... I mean yes, that's his name. So you know that he is the one that was last seen with your mother before she was found overdosed in a hotel then right?"

The more Aunt Juanita sobbed, I just sat there and replayed back to all the times, since I was a teenager all the way up until now, I had seen him. I couldn't believe he had been under my nose this whole time.

I couldn't let him get away, not after all he had done. For his sake, Eddie had better ran out of town. After letting some of the younger soldiers know who I was looking for, I knew someone would find him.

"I got'em cuz. I followed that motherfucker to his house." Lil C said in a whisper through the payphone.

"Oh yea, what side of town he's own?"

"He's on the Southside cuz. But let me do'em... I've itching to put that work in."

"Just meet me at the William Brown's Chicken shack Lil C."

When I met up with Lil C, he gave me a brief run down on how Eddie B usually left out the house at around 10a.m. before I decided to head over his way in my SUV.

"Yea... He done fucked up now cuz. I want to see the white in that niggas' eyes."

While I drove to Eddie's apartment, Lil C was snorting cocaine in-between talking to himself. It sounded more like he was trying to talk himself into following through with what he wanted to do. We arrived so early at Eddie's place that we seen several mothers taking their kids to Sunday school and church.

"Shit a prayer ain't even going save his ass . . . . Rock-ah-bye baby." Lil C said as he cocked and rested the SKS semiautomatic rifle in his lap.

When the apartment's security squad car drove by us making their rounds—I sat there waiting for the parking lot to clear out. I felt as though it was only me in the car thinking with a conscience. I knew that when he came down from his high, he'd realize what he had done. "Alright, there that nigga goes, now all I want you to do since you're here is look out for the cops and yell *Five-O* if any of them pull back around."

"No doubt cuz. I'm going to watch your back too in case he tries to do some slick shit."

Once Eddie B left out his apartment, I crept up on him from the side—for the first time since my first murder; I began sweating as my heart started pumping blood faster throughout my whole upper chest.

WAM WAM!

After striking him with a jaw-piercing hook, I followed it with a jab directly to his nose only to return with a fist full of blood. It was as if he had seen a ghost by the hysterical look he had holding his jaw with both hands causing him to drop his car keys.

SMACK! A solid jab followed by a combination of uppercuts caused his head to turn away from me, as I witnessed a tear fall from his eye.

In the midst of all this, for a reason unbeknownst to me, I felt as if I was at a crossroad in my life at this very moment. The voices started seeming as though they were coming from over my shoulder, then I felt as though I was being watched. I slightly stepped back to scan the perimeter when I checked over my shoulder only to catch a quick glance of Lil C face fixed with a deranged stare.

"Ahh!"

"Why . . . Why in tha fuck did you do it?" I yelled at him releasing all the anger I had pent up inside of me after all these years.

"I never meant for it to come to this man . . . Your mom hated me so much that she said she would deny it if I ever told you. She said she wanted to get off drugs first before she told you."

BOOM! The sole of my foot sounded off as it found the center tip end of Eddies' nose. "You lying mothafucker, you got some nerves. Bitch she died getting high with yo funky ass!"

Just leave him, walk away—this is enough.

I heard the voice come off calm and quietly.

Reaching down to snatch him by the collar of his Members Only leather jacket, I rushed him back and threw him up against his car when I heard someone else's car door shut.

"See, the way I see it . . . You already were dead to me nigga. You think telling me who you are means something . . . Or you thought it was going to change something?"

I said staring into his eyes as though I could see through him. I then noticed that he too had thick eyebrows like I did, as well as hazel eyes like mines. His eyes were fixed bulging back at me as if he didn't know what was going to happen next. He wasn't even worth me killing.

When I threw him to ground before reaching to grab my cap, I glanced back witnessing him reach into his pockets. Everything from there happened so fast.

"Ronnie watch out!"

As I turned back to Eddie to face him, Lil C stood in front of me with his riffle aimed at Eddie who threw one hand up with the other one inside his coat pocket.

"Waiiiittt!"

Blaaaaap Blaaaaap Blaaaaap!

The rounds sounded off like firecrackers echoing throughout the entire neighborhood with the unmistakable sound of an automatic machine gun.

"Whoa . . . . What tha fuck you doing nigga!" I said grabbing the gun out of Lil C hands that still shook after seeing what he had done.

Eddie lay there, twitching uncontrollably as blood squirted from all over his body. The calico shell rounds drew a diagonal streak from his stomach to his left shoulder that was quite atrocious to take in visually.

"I thought he was trying to make a move bra. I told you I got your back." Lil C said while looking in-between Eddie and me before he whispered-

"C'mon man, we got to go before someone sees our faces."

Him telling me that reminded me of what I once told Barry when we were younger . . . I had witnessed too much killing.

As I stared at the bloody mess that Eddie was a victim of, his eyes met mines as his right hand was still inside his coat pocket. I slowly stepped over his body leaning over to see what it was he was actually reaching for. The whole time, his eyes had this sad dismayed look in them.

When I took his wrist out his jacket, he sighed and whimpered as if he could feel some sort of pain still. I couldn't believe what I had seen next, the back of a picture. It was old and the edges were dirty, but it read Christmas 1982.

I flipped it over and lost my breathe. It was a familiar picture of me at the age of five on the top of a bike with a big red bow on it. I had seen this picture around the house and in scrapbooks, but it was torn in half. This one had Eddie smiling from ear to ear while knelling down in front of the bike with my mom standing over him smiling as well.

As I gathered myself, I slowly looked back over to Eddie only to witness him lay there lifeless with his eyes wide open.

HONK HONK!

"Cuz . . . Come on. That nigga dead."

I slowly stuck the only picture I had of the three of us in my pocket and decided that I had seen enough.

Barry

"Close my damn door and get the hell in man."

"What's up B, what's your problem man? I thought we were on good terms ." Detective Kyle said as he put on his RayBan sunglasses, as he didn't want to be picked out meeting with the leader of a criminal organization that his Bureau was investigating intensely.

"You know what the God damn problem is Detective Kyle, or should I say KT! Whoever you want to call yourself," Barry said sitting next to him in the back seat.

"Look nigga, I pay you a salary for information, and that's only because you're useful."

Barry said driving his finger into Kyle's chest. Staring him down, Barry aggressively frisked him at the same time.

"Now when you stop being useful, we will use you as an example. You catch my drift?" Barry said as he withdrew a cell phone from within his coat pocket.

"Aww naw man, we can always do business. You know I'm willing to help you guys as much as I can."

"You fucking mean as long as we're paying you right!"

"Well, first thing first, who in the fuck busted Short Dogg? What's that dudes' name?"

"Uhmm, from what I hear, it was an agent working against the Mobb. His name is Detective Jacobs, but the name that he goes by in the streets is

Jaz." Detective Kyle regretfully admitted knowing that he was putting his coworker's life at stake.

"Humm. Take this phone and tell him that I want to meet up with him personally inside Cutz In Da Hood barbershop in about half an hour."

Why did I even get involved in this shit? I know this man's family. Kyle thought as he remembered the last time he seen Detective Jacobs in the office with his youngest son and wife as it was kids and spouse's day at work.

Barry then whispered for Kyle to put the phone on speaker while he talked to Detective Jacobs.

"Hell yeah Kyle! I'm all over that. I know them and how they move like the back of my hand." Detective Jacobs said in a conceded tone.

As Cap pulled into the car wash Detective Kyle was filled with emotion as he reached to open his door.

"Don't you want your pay Detective Kyle? After all, it only business."

After staring at the bag he declined it with a lump of sentiment in his throat.

"Naw B. I'm done. Consider this my last job for you guys."

Chapter 18

Loyalty Before Royalty

"That means you don't go over that line. Once you go over that line there's no coming back, whether you're a member of the family or not. That's when people get whacked..."   *Loyalty—Cash Money*

Donell

"NAW YOU NEED to just chill and handle business. I'm going to handle this nigga."

"Alright, but once I get done with this I'm coming over." Ronnie assured me before hanging up the phone.

My brother was really starting to appear to be Mr. Untouchable when it came to beating FED cases. From the outside looking in, it seemed as though he was playing all the right cards with the way he positioned himself always staying two steps ahead.

The more game Barry gave me, the more I soaked it up and made moves on my own. I was the face everyone was seeing more and more often. More people could tell that it was me making things happen and I knew this would bring me to the top. And it wouldn't be long after that before I had the power.

It seemed as though the deeper I got into the game, the less hustlers remembered me for playing basketball, which meant they recognized my hustle. Although my brother and I had different ways of spending out money, at times it felt as though we were more like night and day with the money we made and how we chose to spend it.

The most obvious difference between Barry and me was how he wanted to be conceived as a justifiable businesses tycoon. He had a string of legitimate businesses and vocational real estate from Miami to Hawaii. Barry gave off the impression of being lawful to those who didn't take a second look.

I on the other hand knew better and didn't give a second thought about people speculating what I did for a living. After all, I wasn't getting drafted and I damn sure wasn't going to get out the game now. I was too close to being a *real* Boss. Making millions of dollars, driving foreign sports cars and partying with the finest women—I intended to live every day as my last.

I had well over half a million dollars in jewelry alone. From custom charm pieces to studded earring- everything had to be platinum. Rhonda and I even shared a jewelry box that read *platinum plus*. After all the time we'd been together, Rhonda had her bipolar moments when she would do things without thinking. And with my reputation growing in different circles, both Ronnie and Barry said I should cut her off, but the sex was too damn good. Not to mention that she knew our operations like the back of her hand.

Detective Johnson

After getting my haircut, I was surprised to had seen Jacobs pull up into the parking lot. Seeing that he was on a mission, I still decided to speak to him as he went into his trunk.

"It's on and popping now Jacobs, we're official."

"I'm meeting with Stanley and Donell in a minute. After that, it shouldn't be long before I see Barry face to face."

"Then today is your lucky day partner because I'm meeting with Barry and Donell right now and I want you to be there too."

"Wayne, bring yo ass on man, we're falling asleep waiting on ya'll, man." Stanley said standing outside the barbershop door staring at us in the parking lot.

As I followed Jacobs, I couldn't help but notice how relaxed he was.

I mean we were investigating at least fifteen homicide cases from these guys, from kidnapping to shootouts, these dudes are nothing to be taken lightly.

"Relax, Johnson. I got it all under control. I got these niggas in my corner pocket. By the way, I heard him call you Wayne just then. So you go by that name?"

"Yeah," I replied, half nervous while the other half of me was more than ready to make this happen and get it over with.

"You know what Wayne." Detective Jacobs said looking back to me while walking up the stairs in front of him.

"When all this is over with, you got to come to a little league football game with me. My oldest boy is the best running back in Dallas."

Once inside the small meeting room in the back, I noticed Barry wasn't even there, only Donell, JD, Stanley and a slim but muscular dude named Bodei.

"So my nigga, how many guns have you bought from Jaz?" Donell asked me as all eyes were on me looking for me to answer.

"A lot... Some pistols, shotguns, some of everything."

"Well since both of y'all are here, we might as well get straight on down to business." Donell said rising up from the barstool to lean across the pool table.

"Shit, how many guns y'all need now, D? I used to get them for Short Dogg until he got busted, but hell I'm still in business." Jacobs said leaning back against the wall with one leg behind him, resting both his hands on his belt buckle.

"Well first off, I don't shop with nigga's who are suspect."

I looked at Jacobs as he stared back at Donell, screwing his face up at him at the same time.

"Nigga, can't nobody question mines and how I handle business. And if another think he can, he's a mothafuckin' hater." Jacobs retorted.

Watching everything for the smallest sign, out of my peripheral I seen JD arise from his bar stool, and walk toward Jacobs who stood next to me.

"I heard you're working with them, Jaz."

"Mothafucka you-" were the last words Jacobs uttered before JD lunged across me, throwing an uppercut into Jacobs chin that sent him to the ground instantly.

Pushing me aside, JD squatted over Jacobs with his shirt collar in one hand, yanking him off the ground as he threw two more vicious hooks into his jaw.

"Man D, what the fuck is going on, dawg?"

"Chill Wayne, this nigga is a fucking cop!" Donell yelled heated standing over the two with his pool stick underneath Jacobs' chin.

"One of his own gave him up, and said he's the undercover that busted Short Dogg."

"Man, you're out your rabbit ass mind? Show me who said that bullshit and I kill his ass!" Jacobs said spitting blood from his mouth while trying to rise to his feet.

"Oh yeah? Well, then we all must be out our mind motherfucka!" JD said as he lunged back into Jacob, but this time with a switch blade.

He stabbed Jacobs in his ribs, stomach and finally, his jugular.

As I went to stop JD, Bodei quickly drew his gun on me, grabbed me by my throat and pushed me back against the wall.

This shit can't be happening!

"Nigga, you want some too!"

"You got a problem with how we do business? You can die too nigga!" Bodei yelled holding the barrel of his gun in my face.

"Nigga I ain't no mothafucking cop."

"But if you threaten me one more motherfuckin time, you better pull that trigger, because I'm going to pull mine and shoot yo ass next nigga!"

"No!" Donell said stepping aside Bodei as he lowered his arm.

"He's not a cop man, I've sold him dope and it's niggas that vouch for him. It's *this* nigga that Barry said is a cop, not Wayne."

Donell turned to me, and just stared into my eyes.

"If you want to be down all the way, then now is the time."

"Nigga, fuck this shit, I'm here to get paid, not have niggas threaten me with a fucking gun in my face."

Standing next to the door we came in through, I tried not to look down at Jacobs as I could hear his panting in pain. JD coldly stood there looking down at him watching him bleed to death.

"Yeah, mothafucka you gonna die slow nigga."

"Donnie, hand me the piece." JD said, never losing sight of Jacobs all the while.

"Go head and roll out then cuz. We're going to get up with you later on." Donell said withdrawing a pistol from his back that had a silencer on it.

Turning to open the door, I heard three shots mutely fired into my friend's body. I didn't even bother to look back, I had let him down. It all happened so fast and I froze up- I let myself down.

Chapter 19

Blowin' Money Fast

"I'm the best ever. I'm the most brutal, vicious and most ruthless champion there's ever been. No one can stop me. I'm the best ever.
-Mike Tyson

". . . And when I make moves I got a hundred niggas with me Just incase a nigga out there tryin 'a get me . . ."
C-Murder—Down 4 My N's

Barry

BY THE END of '99 I had seen and been through it all; from buying judges, posting bonds to losing drug shipments back to back. And every time, like clockwork, we still managed to keep our operations running smoothly. When situations got sticky, Detective Kyle tried his best to distance himself from the Mobb and me, but I still wouldn't hesitate to put a bounty on his head at the same time.

Nowadays, I could look around me and everyone the Mobb started out with were getting jammed up and getting crazy prison sentences. Baby Blue was raided on Thanksgiving and by Christmas Eve he was sentenced to life imprisonment. Sometimes, no matter how much *pull* I had, I still couldn't be everywhere at once. Going away for a long time can happen a lot sooner than you think when you play the game we played.

It's like everyday you're on top; you're living on burrowed time. Felix and his uncle Carlos were living witness and they knew they were being watched as they warned me when I flew into town last time. I mean there were vans alongside the service road with men taking pictures inside. Some were even talking on handheld radios, not caring if I saw them or not.

Police Commissioner Daniels and Police Chief Atkins were constantly leaking information on who the task force was going to move in on next, and on who was doing the ratting. By now, our whole crew and everyone we knew in South Carolina had been scooped up in one big sweep. Des and Jr. were charged with the largest genocide related crimes the state had ever approached. South and North Carolina murder rate decreased over seventy percent when they were taken into custody. They pleaded guilty so they wouldn't get the lethal injection as their cases made the national news.

Their enforcers, who were childhood friends of Ronnie, were either set up or ambushed and killed. As close as I was with them, the most I could contact them was through letters because everything now was totally turned up; the surveillance, the wires and the informants.

On New Years Eve, to lift everyone's spirits I flew the whole crew to Sacramento to a Cash Money Concert. I mean everybody, from fellas I met in Carolina to players Donell hoped with in college- I just wanted everyone to feel glad about being free.

We drove away from the airport in Sacramento in two stretch limos, with only one stop: the Delta King Floating Hotel. Donell had made the reservations and gone on and on about all the amenities it had, from the two theatres to the restaurant and so on.

Even with a entourage as enormous as ours, Donell insisted that Rhonda not come, and from what I heard through the grapevine, she was highly pissed about it.

When we arrived at the pier of the hotel, we were all high. Talking loud and boasting, everyone was excited about tomorrow night. The Cash Money rappers were the hottest crew out right now.

And as far as the places we went- from the moment we entered the clothing stores, the owners locked the doors so we could buy attire without being watched. From there, we swarmed the VIP sections in strip clubs, buying out the bars and standing on the couches. Wherever we went that weekend, our mob made lines and crowds of onlookers part as if we were moving mountains.

The ultimate splurging moment came when we attended the Cash Money concert at the Arco Arena. I led the pack with Ronnie to my left and Donell to my right, with everyone else behind us dressed in all black. We walked through the arena and made a spot in the middle of the walkway when Juvenile performed *400 Degreez:*

> *You see me I eat sleep shit and talk rap*
> *You see that 98 Mercedes on TV. I bout that*

I had some felonies charges, I bought that . . . .
Nigga disrespect me I'ma be in all black.

As we stood there, wearing an array of different charms and jewelry, from medallions and bracelets to Cartier watches, we sang word for word while holding bottles in the air. Then my night came to an abrupt halt.

Donell leaned toward me, one arm over my shoulder and the other pointing into a discrete crowd of half-naked women. Their fitted and skintight outfits seemed as if they were wearing nothing at all. Then I recognized her.

She had on an all-white silk Vera Wang one-piece bodysuit. It had one silk strap that came from a gold ring around her navel, exposing her pierced bellybutton, that led upward and around her neck. As the strap split into two, covering her breasts, it left her bare back exposed and formed a big circle.

Dancing as if she were in a music video, she used her friends' back for leverage while she poked her butt out. Her ass was bigger than ever and it moved as if it had a mind of its own. Wearing gold Gucci stilettos to match her jewelry, she was absolutely flawless. After three long years I had found my college lover, Brandi Watson.

Standing there in awe of her beauty, I undressed her with my eyes. When her eyes met mine, her jaw dropped. She covered her mouth before running over to me, only to turn around and back her ass up on my pelvis. As we danced nonstop to "U Understand," "Back That Azz Up," "Project Chick," "#1 Stunner" and "Hot Girl," my dick was rock hard.

After exchanging sly remarks in between songs, I could tell she was slightly drunk and so were her friends. Donell and Danny D looked on with lust-filled eyes as they wasted no time easing up behind Brandi's friends for a dance.

"Dayum Boy, you're pretty excited down there."

"I see you still can work the pole."

When we all left the Arena, our crews went to the after party and then to the Waffle House where we stayed until 4 a.m. Brandi and I headed back to the hotel with a bottle of Hennessy and quarter pound of weed. On the way there, Brandi and I made small talk about what we did everyday while headed to my suite. Once there, I began undressing while kissing her aggressively, only slowing down to take my time to lick and tease her nipples. Laying her on her back, I ran my hands through her silky black hair when I caught her admiring my muscular six-pack abdomen. She then looked at me as if for the first time ever, and kissed me softly on my abs while gradually leaning up from the bed. Brandi sucked my bottom lip, hinting to me that she was feeling anxious and horny. In the process of taking her one piece outfit off from over her head, I couldn't help but notice a scar below her navel.

Her pussy was even moister now from all the fingering and foreplay we had done. It was second nature, the way she sat on the edge of the bed and began to stroke my dick while looking at it with an erotic smile on her face.

"Lay down baby. You know what I like." She said patting the bed beside her.

After removing my shirt, she smiled and sighed at how muscular I still was despite the years.

"Thug Passion?" Brandi read aloud, admiring my necklace tattoo as she slowly mounted me allowing her breasts to cause erotic friction between my chest and her Reese's dark brown nipples. She then licked and kissed me from my lips to my chin down to my neck and collarbone. Then she reached back and caressed my hardened penis underneath the condom, then my privates with her fingers while slowly backing down on it. Using my hardened shaft to part her ultrasoft pussy walls only made my dick harder. Brandi slanted eyes rolled backwards before she closed them, taking deep breaths.

She took her time taking all of me inside of her tight walls, while I took the top of her hands and placed them behind her on her ass allowing her to feel how soft it was. "Shit Barry. Yo' dick feel so fuckin' hard."

As she rocked her supple ass back and forward, meeting my long pelvis thrusts, she began to hold on for dear life as her thighs began shaking. From there, she regained her energy only to turn around and ride my dick reverse cowgirl style. I leaned up against the headboard as she used my knees as leverage to bounce her ass up and down while I aggressively rubbed and smacked it. The more she raised her ass up only to slam her ass back down in my lap, the more I could see all the cum that covered my dick like whipped cream. From there we went on and on throughout the night, switching positions and orgasms back and forth.

Detective Johnson

While I rocked back and forth behind my desk, I didn't regret one bit of the argument that led to a shouting match between me and Special Agent Logan.

"I'm going to take you off this case, Johnson! You had better get your shit together!"

"Shit, ya'll motherfuckas can't even get an agent bold enough to risk his neck long enough to get some concrete information!"

Barry was so powerful that he had players killing informants, witnesses and jurors for free, just to get inside their Mobb circle. It became impossible for an Agent to do his initial task: to preserve life. Just coming in contact with him or Bosses who he gave a lot of advice to wasn't worth the risk. And that's how our confidential informants felt.

After making the report of JD killing Detective Jacobs, Logan decided to send me to mandatory counseling sessions as an ultimatum if I wanted to stay on the case. From the sleepless nights I was having to being easily startled, I was diagnosed with Generalized Anxiety Disorder deriving from environmental factors. Although I realized that at times it seemed daunting because I wasn't used to feeling this way, I chose to make the sacrifice.

What was even scarier was how Donell was coming from underneath Barry's shadows and making his presence felt too. When I first started out pursuing their crime ring, I was full of zeal more than anything. But after witnessing my friends and partners fall victim, Logan stated that I had more courage than anything.

Looking at the memorial card from Jacobs' funeral, I still couldn't believe how it all happened so fast. Jacobs was more of a mentor than a partner to me. Since that evening, when I went into the field now, I suspected anything from anyone at any given moment.

"*Those motherfuckas got someone within the Bureau!*"

To hell with taking down this so-called Mafia if I have to die in the process. What good am I dead? Now I wanted more than anything to look that motherfucka Barry and his wanna-be *American Gangster*-ass brother in the face when I testified to the prosecutors that they were indeed the men responsible for the murders and drug overdoses of so many families.

Detective Logan was undoubtedly the best Special Investigation Agent smoking, as far as infiltrating organized crime rings went. He had done undercover work in every shit hole in the system, even Pelican Bay prison.

He gained quite a bit of credibility from taking down drug rings, but even after all his years of experience from the trenches, Logan still was in awe at how Barry could control so many people with different personalities.

"A man like that is his own worst enemy. And if that isn't the case, then his brother damn sure is." Logan would often tell me little details that he learned about Barry and asked me if I needed a break. I declined every time while taking the sessions, as I knew it was mind over matter. Plus, there was no way in hell I was about to let a criminal make me stop doing my job of making neighborhoods safe. I became more driven than ever when Logan and the District Attorney said that Jacobs' death wasn't enough to bring down Barry.

"We can definitely lock his brother up, but it will be as if we're settling for seconds compared to who actually *is* responsible and masterminds the whole organization."

Once I informed Agent Logan that someone was releasing information, he showed me a confidential list of agents around the country that had already penetrated the organization's circle. I only briefly glanced at it, because I didn't know the agents by their real names, only their street names.

"You done went too far now motherfucker." I said heading to the dry-erase board to post some recent pictures our informants had taken of him at the Cash Money Concert.

Chapter 20

Made My bed

"Shit gets deeper, you get the picture . . . ."
Denzel Washington—Training Day(Film)

". . .I'm a cop pretending to be a drug dealer. I ain't nothing but a drug dealer pretending to be a cop. I ain't going to pretend no more.."
Laurence Fishburne- Deep Cover(Film)

Barry

WITH THE WEEKEND coming to an end, Donell mentioned how we spent somewhere close to seven hundred thousand dollars in three days. From first class plane tickets to partying in penthouse suits, we went all out. Even though all of us were from all over, I personally knew each one of them. I never felt as though I was surrounded by people who wanted money, or needed attention- everyone knew everyone and we all did our own dirt, but we were loyal, or at least I thought that.

Even Donell, at one time or another, had done something for someone else in the crew. Such as the time when one of our people got into a heated argument with some hustlers in D.C. during Fourth of July weekend. Outnumbered in the midst of the brawl, he'd ended up getting robbed of his jewelry and his car.

After he and his crew couldn't find out the men who exactly robbed him, he called Donell. Donell was soo upset about the situation it seemed as though he was willing to fly to D.C. and go to war over the incident himself.

"It ain't about the fucking chain and that nigga car, it's about the respect." Donell told me furiously into the phone. This was the first time before many when Donell proved himself as the go to guy as he not only got the mans' car back, but by the end of that same week without a scratch on it, as well as all of his jewelry still in the glove department.

After last weekend, everyone started calling me Don B. *"You're the Godfather my nigga. You're like a Don of this shit . . . I'm proud that I've known you after all this time, you're still a real humble nigga."*

And the list of salutations went on and on out of respect, recognizing that I was the one who came from having nothing to everything, and still made a way for others to do the same for themselves.

As I parted from the crowd to step into a public restroom, I was caught off guard. When I stepped inside the stall, I turned around to shut the door and there he was.

"Don B, huh?" The light skinned brother said as he stared dead into my eyes before withdrawing his wallet to show me his ID. It read *Department Of Investigation, Special Agent William Logan* and in bold letters in the middle, *FBI*.

"You pigs think you got enough to come and fuck with me now?"

"Oh, I know we do, kingpin."

"If you think you do then what the fuck are you waiting for, Will?" I said, taunting him by calling him by his first name.

While I stood there staring back at him waiting for his response, I wondered how long it would be before JD came from outside to see what was taking me so long. I was curious to see the look on Ronnie's face had he seen this pig disguised in regular clothes standing in my way.

"Listen Barry, we want you to stay alive. I personally want to see your facial expression when the judge sentences you to the death penalty. So do us all a favor and keep living."

Pushing him aside on my way out of the stall, my eyes meet with Ronnie's as he immediately stopped and stared down Special Agent Logan. He would have gunned him down if he had a pistol. While Ronnie placed his arm over my shoulder and escorted me out of the now-crowded public restroom, Special Agent Logan stood there gathering his thoughts and was joined by another Agent.

"They're coming for you . . . and it's not us. They're plotting to get you, and especially you, Mr. Marshall." He said looking into Ronnie's eyes as if he knew him.

The last words he spoke really hit home, but I wasn't about to show it. The entire time I kept on my way toward the exit while never breaking a stride. The only question that stayed in my mind was why in the hell does he think Ronnie's name is Marshall?

Donell (Some Weeks Later)

"You mothafuckas got to be kidding me!" Ya'll mothafuckas getting fat off us. Check your pockets, your bank accounts . . . Those zeroes and commas came from the Mobb."

Every since the FBI agents came and met with Barry in the airport in Sacramento, fewer and fewer police wanted to inform us with information surrounding our cases.

"Listen Donell, ya'll are too damn hot." Police Chief Atkins said.

"We'll let you to use our squad cars to transport guns and drugs one last time."

"You may want to watch your back out here as well because some of the business owners that your brother has been extorting are getting bolder, beginning to speaking out against you guys." Police Commissioner Jimmy said while rubbing his chin. "Did I mention that some club owners filed a report on Monday on your organization?"

"Well who the fuck was it Jimmy?"

"You know what…" I said cutting him off in thought.

"You two take ya'll fifty-fifty asses on about your business."

"Ya'll crooked asses aren't even doing your police job and now you can't even do this job. Shit, paying ya'll would be as good as throwing money in the ocean.

"Let's watch how we're talking to one another Donell."

Opening the doors to my Ferrari 430 Spider, I sat there listening to "A Week Ago" by Jay-Z ft. Too Short.

"What the fuck ever man. How bout ya'll just go back to yo' punk ass office, sit behind yo' punk ass desk and die living your punk ass lives?"

I slowly drifted off, thinking about all the dirt I'd done. I felt as though it was time for Barry and me to move our operation to a new city before things got any more out of hand.

On top of that, Stanley was turning into an infection. The more I fed him a large drug deal, the more he wanted to go out and seek players with no street credibility. In the back of my mind, I sometimes thought that he wanted something more—as if he wanted us to get bigger and do our own thang. We had been friends for a decade and I knew money wasn't coming in between us, but sometimes money came in between our understanding.

Barry

Nowadays, things were absurd to the point where I couldn't even go places without changing cars because of who might be following me. The Feds were snapping pictures of my homes, cars and all the friends who came over to my place- everything was just so overwhelming. And on top of that, I was getting calls having to do with Bosses extorting drug dealers, not to mention losing profit from money being seized and raided.

And on top of all that, Rhonda had grown more envious than ever once Donell had came back from California. She was telling her friends the family business and making threats to notify the Feds about where and when our shipments where coming. I personally felt that Donell only made situations worse once he stopped answering her phone calls. I warned him a long time ago to cut her off, and now she was a real problem.

I had to step in because I was the only one who Rhonda acted like she had some sense with. Once I arrived at her condo, it brought back memories off how things were before we all went to college, when we all stayed out of trouble and kept our noses clean.

No one was who they appeared to be anymore. See, word on the street was Lil C had been robbing the Mobb stash houses, but I knew that wasn't his MO. After getting to the bottom of things, I found out that Rhonda had begun snorting cocaine and smoking PCP on the down low. And Lil C was who she scored her powder from, but when she became a regular customer, he put two and two together as to who was really using it. Paranoid that word might get out about her being a junkie, she lied on him, but it was actually her who was caught with her hands in the cookie jar. See women let emotions get the best of them, and drug addicts let their addictions control their lives- put them together and you'll go down with them. But not me and mines I thought shifting the hot shot of battery acid I brought with me.

After a lengthy conversation over to her place, I stood up and threw it on the table nonchalantly, but she didn't notice.

"Okay Barry. That's all I want."

"I just want him to remember what he said and how I deserve him, not some other woman." She said rolling over on the couch before sitting straight up.

"Well I left you some powder in case you know someone who may want it."

"Oh, you know no one around me messes with that stuff." She said looking away from it. But I knew otherwise. "Well I'll just leave it here. I mean you can even sell it, you know?" I said on my way out her condo. A little voice in my head, and a gut feeling was telling me that Donell or myself wouldn't be hearing from Rhonda anymore.

Detective Johnson

This case was hot like lava the way everything was rolling downhill. Kidnappings at one place led to informants later found dead in alleys on the other side of town. I found myself heavily indulging in alcohol as my outlet to keep my head wrapped around what was actually the truth, but what was even harder was trying to lawfully uphold my investigation without being corrupted.

Being right under Donell and Stanley kept me in the loop of all the drug dealing and murders they committed. Whether it was a kidnapping for ransom or me being the getaway driver bearing witness to everything, ever since the crew had came back from California, it became an everyday task not get caught up in the deadly criminal plots that Donell and Stanley were committing.

"Say dawg. You got those guns you're supposed to sell still?"

"Hell yeah… What's up?" I said thinking about the assault rifles in the trunk of my car that I was about to sell.

"Good, since you're driving through here, how bout you stop by on your way and let me check them out?"

"Uh, alright when-"

"Good, meet me at the Swett's Plaza, I'll be waiting for you," Stanley said hurriedly. Right then, I knew something was up. I wasn't sure if he was testing me to see if I would show up or not, but I knew that with everything going wrong, this investigation depended on me so it could keep moving forward.

No time to be scared now.

"Aw, fuck man!" I said in disgust, pulling into the crowed shopping center parking lot. I knew the instant I seen all the foreign cars that something was going down, and I was being sucked into it.

"You got to be fucking kidding me."

Agitated but curious, I rolled down my window to shake the hands of the players who I'd grown acquainted with throughout my investigation.

Before me and all around was an array of tricked-out cars and hustlers that I had delivered drugs to at one time or another since I had known Stanley and Donell. But what made me curious was how these dudes were all hustlers that Stanley supplied and dealt with—as if he had been building a crew in Tennessee without anyone knowing.

"Yo, so you bring them guns Wayne. Me and my niggas want to check'em out, make sure they're good to go before we jump off into this gangsta shit."

"Yo Wayne, come here." Danny D said from afar, as his SUV was parked away from everyone else he stood facing his trunk. "I got something for you and Stanley. Donell told me to stop by and make sure you two were laced." He pulled out two anti-ballistic bullet proof vests as if he didn't want anyone else to see what he was handing me. "This that new shit, they're level three vests. And these right here are level four ceramic plates. There isn't a mothafuckin' thing out there that can get through these."

Trying my hardest to keep a straight face, I was taken back to know that Danny D and Donell had access to this type of merchandise. The FBI didn't even have these vests yet. *These niggas finally got me,* I thought, shaking my head as I knew that Stanley, if not Donell too, were planning on testing me the entire time.

When I took the heavy brown bags containing the vest, Danny asked me a question or two about why there were so many people waiting around in the parking lot. Being that Danny D was more of a close friend to Donell than Stanley, I wasn't surprised when he told me that he didn't know these people and how they weren't with the Mobb. In between watching him leave and Stanley pull up, I found out why I was really there.

It turned out that Stanley was fronting some hustlers in Nashville kilos of heroin that he'd bought from the Mobb, saying they were his. As he keep talking, I thought back to how Donell was always going out his way collecting the money when Stanley wasn't paid, when the real reason behind it was because they thought they were just ripping of Stanley, they never knew who his supplier was. They didn't have the slightest idea that his drugs were from the Mobb. It all made sense now because Stanley wanted hustlers outside of Dallas thinking he was a Boss, but now he was getting over on me.

Here I was riding in the back seat beside a *loyal liar* caught up in the exact same madness I had fought so hard not to be a part of. With the convoy of cars tailing behind us, I just stared into Stanley's eyes, wondering why he insisted I come along once I'd given out all the guns I had brought.

"See Wayne, these niggas think it's a game. But today we're going to show them." He said before turning to face me. "By you being here, I know you're down to roll when all this shit comes together."

"Nigga what shit you talking about? The Mobb got soldiers all over."

"Naw. I'm talking about me finally getting what's mine. See, me and Donell going to be the next kings."

"Kings, huh. Is Donell down with this too bro?"

"Not yet. But he will be, and it's going to be me, him and you when all this is all said and done. You see all them niggas back there, I got plenty more, ready and willing to throw down. And when me and Donell start getting our drugs from this new connect I got in St. Louis, I won't need to worry about being in Barry's good graces. You feel me?"

After Stanley revealed to me his envious plot to be the next kingpin, I realized he'd been obsessed with greed the whole time. Everything Donell and him had been doing this entire time was only because Stanley wanted to take Barry's place. Refocusing my attention on how to make it out of this situation, I tightened the straps on my vest and put my hoody over my head as we arrived at the lavish house where the dealers who owed Stanley stayed.

"Now, I want ya'll niggas to go around the back. I want ya'll niggas to shoot out the side and back windows. Take out those fifty-round magazines and insert the one hundred-round ones. And I want ya'll to go in through the front door before me and Wayne go in."

Listening to Stanley orchestrate his goons showed me how determined they were to get down and how money hungry he really was.

BLAT BLAAT BLAAT!

The machine guns roared through the exterior walls as the shattering glass chandeliers woke the quiet neighborhood. From what seemed like every corner, Stanley's henchmen surrounded the sides of the house in seconds, spraying directly into the windows from point blank range. The entire front lawn was left open as Stanley and his men unloaded countless rounds into the kitchen bay windows, bedroom windows on the second floor, and even shot up the cars and trucks parked in the driveway. Then the moment I had anticipated happening came.

"Cover your ears!"

Pulling down his ski mask, Stanley nodded in the direction of the front door while one of the gunmen stepped from between the trucks and threw a grenade onto their porch.

BOOM!

It's not about being at the right place at the right time, but what you do when you're in that position.

BOOOM! BOOM!

Storming through the front door that was now blown off the hinges after the shotgun shells we'd blasted, we emerged from the smoke wearing ski masks, dressed in all black.

Stanley's .223 literally acted as a machete the way it shredded the man's body who attempted to run to the back, while the ones who weren't already dead crawled in pain, bleeding out their ears. It was as if his crew got a high from all the gunplay, as those who were once on the side of the house ruptured the back door and swarmed the rooms in a matter of seconds, shooting everyone that they had seen running for cover.

Everything happened so fast that there wasn't any time to think, only to react. In the midst of running up the stairs, I heard the faint sound of a door behind me open out my peripheral. Swiftly pivoting in the middle of going up the staircase, I saw the door open and the barrel of a shotgun emerge outward, pointing at Stanley's back while he stood looking around the den. Rushing back down the stairs, I felt my heart skip a beat as I lost my footing when we made eye contact.

BLAAT BLAAT!

I'd squeezed the trigger before being launched backwards onto my ass, when I heard him let off a buckshot round in my direction. It felt like my ass was wedged between the steps. My chest was so fucking hot, burning almost. I instantly began sweating when I opened my eyes to what sounded like a dozen footsteps headed my way. The palms of my hands felt like I had rubbed baby oil on them while my neck had a sharp pain in it.

"Nigga you alright? That motherfucka came out of no damn where." The gunmen said as they stood looking at me like a ghost.

"The buckshot ain't even leave a scratch on this nigga vest." One of them said touching me cautiously.

Reaching for Stanley's hand to regain my balance and stand up, I looked at the dude who I had shot. He had two shots in his forehead, one on top of the other as a result of me falling backwards.

"Nigga, you saved my life. I didn't even hear him behind me. I'm glad you was rolling with me, good looking dawg."

Looking around at the wreckage we had done in between counting the bodies that lay there bleeding left my mind blank. It was as if I was breathing through a gas mask the way I heard every breath I took echo in my mind. After searching the house upside down from front to back, underneath the stove, Stanley's solider found what was owed to him and then some. It turned out that their stash was in the deep freezer with over thirty kilos of heroin and half a million dollars saran-wrapped underneath some broken glass.

"Them niggas must have ran and stashed it in here when they heard the gunshots coming through the window." One said as I made a mental note not to report any of this back at the office. I knew that if I didn't want to blow my cover, let alone this case, I needed to sweep what happened tonight under the rug.

Chapter 21

Blind Sides In Life . . . .

"If you gonna be down with me, Be all the way down with me, or get from around me ."   Mystikal—The Man Right Chea

". . .Your life depends on split second decisions. You bet to do something and you bet to do it now." Omar "J Reid" Epps—In Too Deep (Film)

Detective Johnson

"AWESOME, THAT'S GREAT news." Donell mentioned that he wanted to buy a house and I jumped right on it, telling Donell that I knew a man that would sell homes for drug dealers who were looking to get rid of them for quick cash. Donell bought right into it as he met up with me shortly afterwards with four hundred thousand dollars cash in two large Louis Vuitton duffle bags. Once I requested additional government funding, I called DEA agents in Tennessee to plants bugs in the house so I could deliver the nail in the coffin as far as substantial evidence when it came to convicting him as the Chief Financial Operator and Underboss of the Money Mobb Mafia.

When it came to questions concerning Barry, I tended not to answer because the Bureau had too many leaks. Barry was toying with informants, arranging for them to be knocked off as soon as he got a bad vibe from them. Barry and I hadn't even met face to face yet, but I was getting closer and closer to working beside him as time went by.

All the uncover agents except for myself and another undercover agent in St. Louis had thrown in the towel when it came to working this case. Barry was just too quick to say "Fuck that nigga, kill him." In Baltimore, Barry was believed to have supposedly issued the hit on Tony T—a major established drug dealer who was going in and out of jail and still buying drugs from the Mobb. A victim's former classmate who we had investigated admitted that Barry wasn't sure if he was snitching or not—so instead of getting to the bottom of it, he paid Tony T's girlfriend to set him up so a dude name Calvin Marshall could kill him.

"Yo check it kid. What's so crazy about it is how it all went down."

"His girlfriend volunteered to babysit his daughter that night since she knew that he was going to get killed while at his house, but his daughter left her school backpack at his house. So his girlfriend thought it would be safer to meet him at a bank than to go over his house. But what she didn't know was that he was being followed.

"Calvin Marshall and a fella named JD were following him to the bank in an Astro van as he pulled into the parking lot. When he parked, his girlfriend got out of the car to get the backpack while his daughter lay asleep in the backseat."

"Once he handed her the backpack through the window, he just sat there, talking to her and whatnot. Then all of a sudden the van pulled in front of the cars and a masked man emerged unloading a Tommy submachine gun.

"This dude sprayed Tony T up while he sat behind the steering wheel, still wearing his seatbelt."

"The masked dude also shot his girlfriend up as she stood between both cars with the backpack in her hand. She was shot up real bad from the waist down as the bullets were fired side to side and into the car windshield. He then walked up beside the car to make sure Tony T was dead, and he looked down behind him and saw that the gunshots had woken up his daughter as she sat there hysterically screaming at seeing her father's blood everywhere. His girlfriend is paralyzed from the waist down, but she will tell you the same thing too, officer."

Although I felt as though I should have met Barry long ago for all the work I had done, I knew that I would surely be meeting Barry tonight for the simple fact that I had two million dollars of his. Stanley was initially supposed to pick it up, but Donell said I could do it since I had been doing the same thing for them all along. Even though I was only delivering the money to him it meant more than just that to me because I had been anticipating this moment for well over a year now.

After Donell alerted me as to what to do with one half of the two million dollars, he mentioned how Detective Kyle was going to send the remainder of the money to the Cayman Islands. "Don't be shocked neither Wayne, that nigga is a FED. He a crooked agent that Barry been paying off the whole time."

I couldn't believe that the Mobb had a mole within my division, let alone in the same Bureau. I mean we're supposed to be taking bad guys off the streets, not helping them take out our own kind.

"Yeah yeah, I know right. I was surprised when I met that nigga too. We been using him to keep us three steps ahead, so don't mess with him. Just give him the dough alright. Stanley told me how ya'll turned the lights out in Tennessee and the last thing I need yo ass doing is killing this nigga too."

Donell may have found it loyal of me to kill that man and save his friend's life, but if only they knew how often I wanted to shoot them too. Even though I knew what I did wasn't right, it had to be done for the sake of this case. And if me protecting myself appeared to be loyalty to their organization, then so be it.

Ronnie

It was as if a light bulb went off in my head when I placed two and two together. The guy behind the shades with the hoody on his head the day Short Dogg was busted was Wayne!

I knew something wasn't right with that motherfucka, I thought to myself while I got into my Corvette and headed to the nightclub that Barry was supposed to be at.

Just as I was expecting, it was crowded as hell in the parking lot with all the club-goers. The only faces that looked familiar were some young and wild goons that Lil C had warned me to watch out for. Even after the incident with Eddie B, Lil C always warned me of players in the city who he couldn't trust. Thinking back to why I had come here, I pulled my ski mask over my face while withdrawing my Desert Eagle, slowly walking past small circles of people in the crowd. It was then when I spotted Barry walking with Wayne by his side.

Detective Johnson

The thought as to whether or not Detective Kyle had blown my cover wrestled in my mind a hundred times since Donell told me over the phone earlier.

Passing by half-naked women eyeing us down trying to get Barry's attention, we stopped and stood in front of his SUV. That's when he began to explain why we were just now meeting, but at the same time I caught this eerie feeling that he'd already *made* me made and was stalling.

"Yeah man, we should have met a long time ago, but I had to check your credentials first, you know. The same niggas that's gangsta in front of you are the same ones that turn right around and turn government informants." He checked his beeper that started going off.

BAP BAP BAP!

Three shots rung out of the man's nine millimeter pistol, hitting Barry once in the shoulder, just inches above my collarbone, before I grabbed Barry and forcefully brought him to the ground.

"Stay down!"

BOOM BOOM BOOM!

My .40 Glock pistol sounded as I returned fire, hitting the shooter twice in his chest and once in his stomach. Barry then leaned back against his SUV, withdrew his .45 Magnum and aimed it at the other shooter's head.

BAT BAT BAT!

Just as soon as the bullets pierced his skull, the man's brains and blood squirted out onto the people who were beside him. Then I realized it was a set-up.

BOOM BOOM BOOM!!

Shots erupted just millimeters from behind my earlobe as I witnessed the third shooter get airborne onto the hood of his car from the shots fired behind me. My adrenaline skyrocketed before I began having shortness of breath when I realized that I'd fired off my last round in the midst of the shoot out.

"AW SHIT! HOLD UP!" I yelled in a desperate plea, not once blinking at the masked shooter holding the warm barrel of the steel gun between my eyes.

"Bro! Chill!" The heat and gun smoke flaring onto my forehead halted my thoughts as I froze in the kneeling position.

"Chill my nigga, he saved my life!"

"Those mothafuckas tried to *ice me* man. Out here in front of *everybody*. Can you believe that shit!" Barry said heatedly to the masked man while looking over at the three dead men across from us.

Women's stilettos echoed as cars skidded to flee the scene. All the while the masked man stood towering over me with his gun hovering above my head. I slowly rose to my feet, but he never took his eyes off me, as if he knew who I *really* was.

"Yo, if this nigga ain't a fucking cop, then I'll be Goddamned!"

"What the hell are you talking about?"

"Look B! It's a cop in our circle, that's selling us out! I saw this nigga raid Short Dogg's house."

Shit. My thoughts began racing. With Barry standing between us, I raised my gun once he lowered his.

It's fucking over, I thought, right when Barry yelled out, "It's that nigga Kyle! He's a crooked undercover. It had to have been him, bro. He's a Fed and Wayne is supposed to see him tonight. It has to be him dog, he's the only person that's suspect. He's waiting beside the Little World convenience store in a white Crown Victoria sedan. We were supposed to give him some money to send away, but I want you to send his ass away for good." Barry said, pointing his index finger into the man's chest.

"He's a dead mothafucka," The masked man mumbled as he jogged back to his Corvette around the same time I heard sirens coming from the freeway.

Damn, that could've been Calvin Marshall, I thought to myself, as I realized that he had me all figured out and didn't even know it.

Chapter 22

Thug Passion

"... Before they hurt you, Read they body language, 85% communication non-verbal, 85% swear they know you, 10% you know they story, man the other 5 . . . time'll show you, just know you".
                                    Beanie Sigel—Feel It in the Air

Ronnie

DRIVING MY LINCOLN **Navigator**, I couldn't help but think back to the last time I visited Louisiana with Barry and Donell. We were always doing something for one another, trying to outdo the other. Whether it was some flashy jewelry Donell bought us, or the latest cars that Barry had shipped to our houses, we didn't compete to show others up, we more so competed to outdo one another when it came to gifts. So when I decided to take them on a trip to the boat casino and then onto a cruise ship, I was going to top them both.

Thinking back to the incident in the parking lot, I hadn't shot anyone up until then. And even before that, after the whole ordeal having to do with Eddie B, I had stopped hearing the voices and having nightmares all together. I found it easier to relax now, not having to look over my shoulder. Even though the numbers of Mobb members getting busted grew every week, the conversations between me and Christina kept me leveled. My mentality and thoughts were going opposite directions compared to everyone else's. Like when Barry mentioned that he was planning a getaway for the Mobb Bosses, I was contemplating going away myself, permanently.

I remember when the three of us were at the Bally's Bella Riverboat Casino. Donell recognized a Latino man accompanying Felix and Carlos at the Roy Jones Jr. versus Reggie Johnson prize fight. At the same time, I saw Antroine whom I was on lockdown with back in the day and decided to make my way over. I later learned that the Latino man made Antroine his bodyguard instead of just another triggerman. Once Antroine introduced us all, we quickly learned that his friend was greater than we could have ever fathomed. Using the port docks of Louisiana as his base, he had pallets, bails and even submersible narcotic submarines overflowing with cocaine, heroin and marijuana for a price twice as cheap as Carlos. With a personality that was more outgoing than any cartel drug lord I'd met, he often went out of his way to smuggle his shipments to us when the Feds applied pressure.

After the fight, Christina was overjoyed to ride the cruise boat for our first date. From Miami to Venice, Italy, the smile on her face and the happiness in her voice was something I'd never seen before. She was on cloud nine and so was I, as I realized then that getting out the game was the answer. It was the answer to the voices I used to hear, the nightmares I had, and the decision that neither of my parents could choose.

Arriving at my hotel not far from Grambling University, I was deep in thought about all the different conversations Christina and I had. Since the cruise boat trip, I really started to grow fond of her genuine personality. She looked like a model but acted more down to earth than anything. She was humble about everything, including her background as well as her upbringing. The way she presented herself after all she'd been through drew me closer to her.

Tonight didn't surprise me one bit when she walked out her apartment looking better than ever in a lavender Juicy Couture spaghetti-strap dress that stopped well above her knees, revealing her toned thighs and plump breasts. Patiently waiting, I sat behind my tinted windows waiting for her to walk down the stairs.

"All you have to do is act like you don't want to have sex and she's definitely going to let you hit it bro." Donell told me on the way here.

"Hey baby."

"What it do baby girl."

Shifting the gears as I merged into the city traffic, Christina began lip singing to my radio.

"Oh so you can sing too?"

"Oh yeah, but I really like rap, the hardcore rap." She said snapping her bubble gum while checking herself in my mirrors.

Taking the initiative, I put in Easy-E's *Easy-Duz-It*. Once she heard the little girl come over my speakers, she immediately snapped out of her train of thought, looked out the window and started mimicking the lyrics:*"What the fuck is up? In the place to be. Coming on the mic is Eazy Mothafuckin-E. Dre is on the beat. Yella's on the cut. So listen up close while we rip shit up."*

She recited while holding her hand still and moving her fingers. I couldn't help but break out into laughter at her. On the cruise I was nervous around her, but now I felt comfortable letting my guard down around her. After dinner and a trip to the Manship theatre, we made small talk as she told me plans for her future. By the way she was wrapped up underneath my arm, I knew she was enjoying herself.

Back at her place, I smoked a blunt and had a few sips of some codeine mixed with Sprite that relaxed my nerves with being over a woman's' house in a city I didn't know. In the corner of the couch with my eyes trained on her, I grew more and more horny watching her walk around wearing her red silk Victoria Secret lingerie set smelling like Jessica McClintock body lotions that made her skin look glossy.

Drinking pink Moscato on the opposite side of the couch, Christina listened to DMX "How's It Goin' Down" while nodding her head to the drums. From tasting her breast to her clit, I thought about going all the way in with her tonight. I had never gone down on a woman before, but when I was locked up, the older cats would talk about it as if it really drove the women crazy. I didn't know if it was the weed or the drinking, but she was driving me wild and by the end of tonight, I was going to drive her up against the wall if not the headboard.

"Ron baby... When we went on that cruise liner, the more I was around you, the more I realized that I had feelings for you a lot stronger than I thought I should. And I didn't want us to have sex then because I didn't want you to think I was *a jump off*."

"And after all I've learned about you, I know better than to think you would be that type of woman."

"All I'm saying is that after all this time, my feelings for you have grown." She said as she slid down the couch I was on, positioning herself directly on top of me while straddling my lap.

"Well the feeling is mutual baby."

"Ronnie baby..." she whispered as she leaned forward to kiss me, pressing her breast against my chest. I felt her wet tongue on my lips as she gently eased it inside my mouth. She tenderly placed her hands on the sides of my temples as she held my ears in her hands and kissed me aggressively. While she sat in front tongue kissing me, I grabbed her waist and massaged her ass cheeks bringing her closer to me. She then unzipped my fleece hoodie and lifted my white muscle shirt to kiss my upper chest, then my six pack.

As if she were in a hurry, she rose up out of my lap, got on her knees and just sat there as she slowly pulled her long hair behind her head into a ponytail. Pulling down my pants, she rolled her tongue out showing me her tongue ring, making my dick harder than it had ever been as I felt it jumping like it had a heartbeat of its own.

"Hold up baby, let me get something real quick."

She walked to the freezer and then back over to the sofa, smiling while looking down at my dick that was now fully hard. She put a little ice in her mouth as she took the majority of my dick in her mouth and acquired a rhythm that slowly sped up.

"Aww... Shit!"

I threw my neck back in bliss at the cold and warm feeling. I felt her jaws squeezing my hard dick while she licked my dickhead with her tongue. I stretched out my arms beside me as she got comfortable on the floor. After taking it as long as I could, I motioning for her to stop and rise up.

As we both stood up, her nipples stood erect as I gradually leaned over to the side and swiftly, in a single motion, picked her up from her waist by grabbing her ass and lower back. Now holding her upside down with my dick in front of her face, she picked up where she'd left off at as she gently grabbed my dick with one hand and took me in her mouth.

After licking the outside of her clit, followed by a series of gentle tongue kisses inside her pussy, I sat her down on the couch and positioned her doggy style. Caressing her supple ass then roughly gripping her cheeks, she turned her face back toward me, watching me guide my dick into her.

"C'mon baby." she said seductively, arching her back up with one foot planted on the floor and one knee on the couch.

"Damn, baby."

The more I slid my shaft into her tight opening, the more her pussy lips spread, making my dick disappear into her wetness. Filling her completely to the point where she couldn't maneuver, she began to grip the sofa while holding her chin down, trying to fight the feeling of ecstasy. Focused attentively, I spread her ass cheeks with both hands as I gripped and brought her soft ass toward me. She then began to close her eyes and shake her head as if she was saying *no* in a silent tone.

"Oh daddy, I can't take it no more." Whispering underneath her breath after every thrust and stoke, I raised my right leg up going deeper as I began pulling her hair. Once I began smacking her ass telling her to give it to me before I take it, she slowly started a rhythm of going back and forward, while at the same time reaching back with her two middle fingers to rub my balls.

"I can feel you in my stomach."

When she deeply sighed from coming, her slippery inner walls began contracting around the skin of my dick as her body stretched out before she collapsed along the edges of the sofa. With sweat dripping from both our bodies, I decided to shower and go on to bed afterwards, as I planned on waking her up with some morning sex before I headed back to Dallas the next day.

Chapter 23

Taking The Backseat . . . .

"Let me give you some very expensive advice, go someplace where you can stay out of trouble."   -King Of New York

Barry

BRO . . . I GOT you, I'm going to find them. You just lay low. You got to keep some sort of clout around you too because we're the top dawgs."

"Yeah, yeah...You're right, I'm not going to let 'em check me, D."

Still pissed about the shoot out, I shoved my clothing into my Louis Vuitton luggage. To my surprise, Donell was the only voice of reason when I came up empty-handed as to who sent those gunmen. These days, I didn't have give Donell too much advice on how to move and anticipate what's next anymore because he carried himself like a Boss now.

Just as Donell's name rung bells in the streets, so did Carlos and Felix as word was out everywhere that they had been apprehended by the DEA. I received confirmation from my lawyer about how their entire organization had been under surveillance for years while the Feds built a stronger case.

"Just turn your television on CNN or Fox Four news and you can't miss it."

I already knew that the Mobb was on the Feds radar and there wasn't no denying it. And after the all the murders, drugs and now the attempt to take me out, I was fed up. Fed up of having to watch what I said on the phone and fed up of having an entourage of cars and men surrounding me. Every since that night, I realized that everything I was putting up with, wasn't even worth it. Although Donell didn't know it yet, my next move would be changing my lifestyle. Beginning today, I was intending to slip right under the Feds noses and catch a flight to Boca Raton, Florida.

Brandi and I had been talking frequently since that unforgettable weekend in Sacramento. Our chemistry picked up as if we had never gone our separate ways. She listened to me and didn't question me. She didn't judge me for the decisions I made, but instead helped me to deal with things that I had to go through. There was just something different about her now. Her voice sounded so tender, nurturing almost. She was patient just as much as she was understanding.

Once I was done packing, I planned on having Ole School, a delivery driver for Domino's Pizza, drive me to the airport. Short Dogg happened to be his nephew, and I'd decided to hire him for odd jobs. Watching him through my mini-blinds as he drove up into my front courtyard, I waved for him to pull around to my five-car carport so we wouldn't be seen. All my homes were in gated communities, and this one in particular was rather far from the street, making surveillance of my residence almost impossible.

"Just set the pizza in the oven."

"Yo son, it was like two vans, two unmarked cars and a squad car parked down the street from this place."

Ole School drove a Lincoln Towncar that was roomy enough for me to stash my luggage inside of without being forced. I couldn't believe I was making millions of dollars a week only to sneak out my own damn home just so I could go somewhere without being hassled. I never saw any of those Italian Mobsters doing this shit in the movies.

What part of the game is this? I thought to myself before I climbed inside the trunk.

"You ready, fam?" Ole School asked as he walked to the trunk of the car with a fire blanket in his hand, anticipating putting it on top of me before I rolled over on my side in between the subwoofers and luggage.

"Make sure you turn the radio to a news channel, then up loud enough so I can hear it alright."

"I gotcha fam."

Slowly driving down the street, I heard him switching the radio stations while reciting the song "Rapper's Delight" to calm his nerves. A whole week and a half had passed since I had gone to Rhonda's condo, and Donell had been blowing my beeper and cell phone up nonstop. While waiting for Ole School to find the radio station, I heard his break pads squeaking a little too soon.

"Yes officer, do you need something?"

"Yes, actually I do. I'm ATF Agent Brass and the gentleman beside me is DEA Agent Tyler, and I'm going to need you to please step outside your vehicle as Agent Tyler searches your car while I ask you a few questions."

"Sure…Officer."

I then heard the Agent drill Ole School with questions such as who was in my house, how many people were in there with me, and if he smelled drugs or saw any guns in my house. I just calmly lay there as he answered *no* to all his questions, while the other one rocked the car, turning over everything that wasn't bolted down.

It wasn't until he hit the trunk release button that I started to get nervous. Listening to his feet shuffle toward the trunk, my heart started beating faster, especially when the agent removed the fire blanket, revealing my expensive luggage.

"Hey Bryan, come here."

"Whoa, Mr. Jenkins, this sure is some expensive luggage to be in the trunk of a pizza guy's car."

"Oh well, Officer, that isn't even real."

"Oh really?" One of the agents said sarcastically.

"Yeah, see look Officer, this shit is all knockoffs." Ole School said before violently kicking my suitcases. "You know it's easy to get phony stuff like this in Brooklyn."

"Mr. Jenkins, I'm going to check your luggage. Now before I begin, is there anything you have to tell us, because now is the time to come clean. Understand?"

While I waited for his response, I felt as though my sense of hearing increased. I heard leaves swaying in the wind and birds chirping from a distance, all the while waiting for the response Ole School would give him.

"Man ain't nothing in there but clothes." He said as the agent wasted no time opening one suitcase then emptying it onto the concrete. When my clothes began hitting the ground, there was absolute silence.

What the hell is going on? Why are they so damn quiet?

The agent took out yet another suitcase.

"Well Mr. Jenkins. We apologize for the inconvenience, and we aren't going to hold you up any longer."

While Ole School loaded my luggage back into the trunk, I lay there still tense but at ease as he continued driving, tuning finally to a news station.

Thursday night ended a twenty-eight month long investigation into a complex human smuggling, drug and money-laundering case. Federal Agents and Immigration say Dallas, Houston and Laredo were a hub for major drug activity, while Laredo was used as a—and I quote—a port for human smuggling. Cooperating together, Federal, State and local agencies are working hard to stop the flow of drugs pouring into our city.

In a multi-agency effort named "Operation Sonar", the FBI placed over twenty-five people in jail from several Mexican drug cartels such as the Sinaloa, La Familia and the Gulf Cartel, including their notorious drug lord Carlos Hernandez and his younger nephew Felix Hernandez, who now faces the death penalty as well as federal charges for their involvement in continuing a criminal racketeering enterprise.

Detective Johnson

I was grateful to God that I was getting to the point of actually breaking this case. From the murders to the parking lot shootout, I was living on the edge both mentally and physically.

The hazard duty incentive pay wasn't hardly enough for what I had to go through. From second guessing my chain of command motives to having nightmares of the people I had either killed or seen killed, I was turning into my own vulnerability. I began taking medicine three times a day just to calm my nerves enough to sleep.

With Det. Kyle was still posing as an undercover, I knew my cover could be blown any day. I realized I couldn't trust anyone anymore. I now took it upon myself to collect as many additional wiretapped conversations and pictures I could. Most importantly because I wanted the extent of the circumstances I was in to be clearly justified, beside the initial purpose which was so that I could link the brothers to the federal crimes they were committing.

Barry, on the other hand was a criminal-minded thug. He didn't depend so much on all the musclemen he had, but the mental manipulation he used on everyone. He patiently played mind games with his calm and decisive reasoning when he saw people who were vulnerable. I learned why the Bureau regarded him more as a prodigy than just another cocaine kingpin.

Barry ran circles around field agents and confidential informants, as well as myself, by the way he did everything so sporadically. I learned quickly that he would let me do most of the talking, while he listened to me ramble on about the things I said I had done. He never admitted to anything or directly asked for anything. It was as if he was scrutinizing everything I said, waiting for me to say something that didn't sound right.

Barry's way of thinking outsmarted those he surrounded himself with. And if he wasn't respected for his mentality, then JD or Calvin Marshall were never too far away to put things in perspective. JD had become so notorious in the underworld that he received one hundred percent of the money for a hit upfront. I removed Ronnie's name as a priority in this investigation, as a man named Calvin Marshall proved to be the third person in their circle. I had a direct order to bring Calvin down the moment I saw him, but that chance had come and gone. Since Logan maintained tactical control, he dispersed field agents to find any information on Marshall, whether it be photos, gossip or via the phone lines we were monitoring, but he only became more frustrated as they all returned empty handed.

Somewhere Across Town . . .

Detective Kyle reminded Bodie of Cuba Gooding Junior acting in the movie *Boyz in the Hood* by the way he thought he could just get out of a situation. Once Ronnie had given Benny and himself the green light to take out Detective Kyle, his life had been as good as a three-dollar bill.

It had been four months since the death of Detective William "Chaz" Jacobs and the SW Regional DEA Bureau believed it to be another murder ordered by the Money Mobb Mafia. Detective Kyle was glad to hear this on the news, which meant that there weren't any signs that could be traced back to him.

Every since he had told Barry the identity of Detective Jacobs, he had purposely put more distance between the Mobb and himself. And with Intel on their enforcer Calvin Marshall circulating, he was glad that he keep his distance from everyone as he continued to stay at his Aunt's house.

"What the fuck?" Detective Kyle mumbled, staring into his rearview mirror only to witness the GMC Denali pull up out of nowhere, blocking him in the driveway. It all seemed like something out of a movie, as the two men speedily exited the SUV. Dressed in black with white face paint, the two men carried extended clip assault rifles, one behind the other, to opposite sides of his car. Locking his car doors, while at the same time cranking his windows up, he checked his rearview mirror as the morning sun glare blocked his vision and he saw a body in his peripheral view.

BLAAP BLAAP BLAAP!

"AHH!" Detective Kyle yelled in pain as his felt the full metal jacket calico bullets penetrate his ribcage as well as his arms and top left shoulder. Posing as a sharpshooter, Bodie unloaded the AK-47 one hundred round magazine through the driver's side door. Doing the same only with a MP-15 and standing at about six feet from the car, Benny shot through the back passenger side.

As the residents' cars still dripped with morning dew, there was not one witness who saw what took place. Detective Kyle's body went from jerking and twitching from the trauma of the abundant bullets to falling sideways onto the armrest, lifeless. He was left with over seventy-eight bullets in his body and over one hundred and twenty rounds in his car.

Detective Johnson

As I exited the freeway, the thought of how long Detective Kyle had been working for the Mobb wasn't what bothered me the most, but how many of the informants and agents working this case he'd given up in the process. After debating with myself and arguing with my psychologist, I realized that my life was at stake everyday I allowed Detective Kyle to be in the field instead of in prison. Although I pondered how much dirt he had on me as leverage, it was worth the risk because at least I would be alive.

After a sit-down with Logan, he decided to send his close friend Jim Reed to accompany me in taking Detective Kyle downtown. Reed knew this was a case that would go down in the books as a head turner as far as the Bureau was concerned. Working in cohesion to apprehend Kyle, we intended to take him into custody hoping he would confess his inside knowledge of the Mobb in exchange for some sort of immunity on the charges we were about to bring up against him.

Driving in between the narrow streets in search of the right house, we were almost sideswiped by a Denali with tinted windows as the driver drove in a hurry down the residential street.

"That son of a bitch knows their driving too damn fast. There's kids going to school."

Even though we were almost in a head-on collision, I was more focused on the numbers on the houses, in search of Detective Kyle's when I saw a little girl in her school uniform stop walking and start screaming as she stared into a driveway.

Chapter 24

Catching Up On Old Times . . . .

"Oh Biggie gimme one more chance I got that good d*ck girl, ya didn't know"   Notorious B.I.G—One More Chance

Barry

FLORIDA WAS ABSOLUTELY beautiful. I flew into Palm Beach International Airport to meet with Brandi later on that night, and I felt liberated. Since it was the Fourth of July weekend, it was crowded everywhere. People of different races covered the sandy beaches, but the sunny weather made everything that much more relaxing. Kingston's Lieutenant, Big Pete, drove me from the airport to my condo downtown in Minzer Park. I owned condos and Villas all throughout Florida. From Orlando to South Beach, I had quite a bit of vacation properties that I leased out to *out of towners*.

"Don B, it's good to see you again man. Kingston is always talking about how you guys been tight since the beginning of time."

"Yeah man, he's been down with me long before I even got into the game."

Arriving at my place around noon, it felt good to be in a city where my neighbors and the majority of people in the city didn't know who I was or what I did.

"Yo man, my crew and I won't be far. We got a hotel about ten minutes from here. I'm going to get some food and then I'm going to come back here and shadow your girl's car while ya'll are out and about tonight. I got three other cats I brought up here from Miami with me and we're all strapped, so if you need us, just beep me." He said as he reached his hand back to shake mines' before I exited the backseat of his Mercedes S550.

Once inside my condo, I showered and waited for Brandi while I thought about how long it would take for her to drive here from her job in

Orlando. In the midst of all this, I checked my voice messages only to hear Donell twice.

The first was in an agitated tone, asking me where I was because I wasn't in Dallas, and the second one was a follow up of him calling me saying that Rhonda was found in her condominium dead from a hotshot of heroin. Neither Donell nor anyone else had a clue of my whereabouts because I never told anyone that I was leaving the city for a week.

I had beach houses in Maui, Puerto Rico, and Key West along with a string of condos in California and Florida. I had been doing everything Uncle Billy told me to the T. I stopped talking on the phone back in '98 and I stopped writing little notes to myself in '99. Now it was the summer of 2000, and I was about to put everything in my rearview mirror and just disappear. I had royalties coming in from business owners and monies from the tenants who rented out my homes. I could have gotten out the game six months ago when I thought about it, I mean I was set for life and then some.

Although half the homes I received monthly income from were being leased out in Wayne's name, he never questioned me. I found his loyalty invaluable because a lot of soldiers grew resistant to doing things once the Feds started locking people up. In between thinking of Wayne's loyalty and about the friends who had turned into informants, there was a coded knock on the door.

"Hey baby." Brandi said with open arms, embracing me. From inside my foyer, I stood in awe of how beautiful she still was. Her hair was curled, falling well past her shoulders revealing her black BeBe halter top and rose petal-decorated dress. Closing the door, I leaned up against it overwhelmed by her Nascar curves and how her Nestle cocoa brown skin glistened.

"You looking good baby."

"Matter of fact, can I go on the record now by saying that all the words that describe 'gorgeous' in the thesaurus are an understatement when it comes to how good you're looking right now."

"I only hope you're feeling that way by the end of the night Barry." She said innocently.

"How bout while we're on our way to your car, you tell me why I wouldn't be."

Scouting the area outside, I spotted Pete's Mercedes parked under a palm tree with the driver's window rolled half way down. Opening her door on the driver's side before getting in myself, we talked about everything under the sun as we went to eat dinner at P.F.Chang's. From there, we went to Red Reef Park and walked along the beach for a few hours to watch the fireworks while she enlightened me about her friends' and family's wellbeing, along with her job as the Regional Supervisor for the Waldorf Astoria Hotel and Resorts.

"So you're living your dream of managing a world famous hotel now aren't you?"

"Something like that, but this is just the tip of the iceberg. I really would like to own my own realty company with condos and beach houses all over the world. I would call it *Presidential*." She said with enthusiasm.

Over the course of us talking on the phone ever since Sacramento, feelings started to resurface on both ends and, at this point in my life, those feelings didn't bother me. I could look into her eyes and see how she was still very much into me for who I was, not who I had become. She still had the same twinkle in her eyes. Her cheeks still swelled up when she blushed, as if this was our first date all over again. I could see it all in her eyes, her facial expression and the tone in her voice: she still loved me now just as much as she had in college.

Walking back to her car, she detoured inside a restaurant close by to use the ladies' room when I received a call on my phone from Donell.

"Wassup."

"Our little league team took a loss today. The white shortstop on the opposing team ran for a homerun this morning." Donell spoke in code, letting me know that the Mobb had just gotten robbed of a good amount of money.

When he said our opponent I knew he meant that the cops stole our money, but when he said "the white shortstop," I knew he was referring to Police Chief Atkins. We made soo much money nowadays that for every thousand dollars, we would say a hundred dollars.

"Damn."

"Well, let me know how bad they got beat, and we will work something out from there." I said before hanging up.

As soon as I put the phone in my pocket, Brandi strolled over to me, all the while staring into my eyes before planting a tender kiss on my lips. After closing her door, I received a text that read *two hundred and fifty* followed by a pound sign.

Detective Johnson and Special Agent Logan

"So are you aware that our friend has left the city Agent Johnson?"

"Yes, I am, sir." I said looking over the sealed indictment documents I'd received.

"Well, if you're the lead detective, I think you should stay on top of these things. You definitely don't want to be remembered for the wrong reason if you drop the ball on this."

"I'm all over it, including the group of people plotting against his crew."

"Well we're up on the wire too, so you know we hear everything." He said conceitedly.

Well that's good, considering that these people weren't up on the phone lines we were monitoring simply because of the fact that these people weren't into any illegal business at all, being that they were legitimate businessmen.

The most mind-blowing information I had discovered came once I intercepted the assault and battery reports from the Police Commissioner's desk. I learned that the same business owners who Barry and Donell were extorting had turned around and put a bounty on their heads, as well as their right hand men such as myself and other fellow agents who had already been found slain. There was a two-hundred and fifty-thousand-dollar ticket for the person who killed Barry, Donell, JD and Ronnie. Detective Kyle knew of this hit the entire time, but didn't mention it because he figured the business owners were doing him a favor.

I knew it was only a matter of time before that crooked mothafucka got straightened out. That's exactly what his ass gets for playing with fire. Hell, for all I knew, he was gonna set me up sooner or later.

Barry

In front of a fireplace built into the wall of my bathroom, Brandi and I shared a chronic joint while watching *A Thin Line between Love and Hate on* the twenty-seven inch TV monitor that rested above it. From the scented candles and colorful display of the rose petals in the jacuzzi, I continued to think of the life we could have lived if I'd never gotten into the underworld.

"When we were in Sacramento, I saw a scar below your bellybutton and

I didn't think nothing of it because I was high and drunk, but now I see it again. Is that because you had a caesarean section?"

Slowly placing her elbow on the ledge, exhaling the smoke from the joint, she began to speak. "When you left me at the airport, I didn't know how to tell you. I was young, scared, and undecided. Unlike you, my mind wasn't made up on anything or anyone else but you. After you walked out on me, I came to find out that I was three weeks pregnant. I was pregnant and you weren't there for me. You were gone and didn't want to be found." Tears began to roll down her face.

"After you changed your cell number, I figured that you didn't want nothing to do with me anymore."

"I seen Joe Joe once at the mall, and he said that he'd tell you that I said to call me—but I see now that he never did." She paused and took another deep breathe. "We have a son Barry, and he looks just like you. From when his eyes open until when he closes them at night. I have a piece of you that will never leave me. I searched for a way to tell you since we met in California, but I just didn't know how."

I kissed her and passionately and took her into the bedroom to make love to her until she fell asleep on top of me. I just laid there, deep in thought.

I got a son ?Does he have wavy hair like me? Is he smart in school?

Although I couldn't sleep, I pretended to, as I was now at another crossroad with a decision to make that I'd never once seen coming.

"I make you smile
but you'd rather have what makes you cry
say goodbye and leave now
with my heart on my sleeve
memories what I found is you
still care you had feelings
and they're still there baby
girl keep it real here
are you still down . . ."

Chapter 25

Keep Your Head On The Swivel . . . .

"My reply for any questions asked, The Devil made me do it. Who's the Devil may I ask? It's so polluted Up-rooted from all this stupid shit . . ."   Pastor Troy—Vica Versa

Donell

I SURE AS HELL hope Barry's having fun going here and there while the Mobb takes heat from every corner, I thought, realizing how I was catching flights three times a week from St. Louis to New York and Louisiana making sure all the monies were accounted for. I began showing my face more and more now.

When money wasn't short from dealers, it was intercepted. Although Barry couldn't have had a clue as to who was responsible for doing this and that, I knew I could as long as I kept my eyes on everyone. I learned with everything going on, I could never be too far away from the action. In order to keep players in line, I had to always be close. Especially after what happened to JD and the attempted hit on my brother, I didn't ride anywhere without having backup.

When I thought back on what my pops and I'd talked about over the phone, I saw he was always right. He was always telling me that before I could be the man, I had to walk a mile and a half in their shoes. I had to know how to function as one before I could hold that number one spot. He would mention how even though Barry was the main man, all I had to do was be patient. *Timing is everything*, he would remind me over and over.

I thought of what my pops would have wanted me to do when it came to urging Barry to stay behind the scenes because local law enforcement had him under twenty-four hour surveillance. Barry anticipated this, and as he had already been right about everything so far, he still couldn't have had a clue as to how much the streets would be filled with the Feds. We were labeled as the multi-million dollar Triple Threat; Barry was the Michael Jordan, JD was Dennis Rodman and I myself was Scottie Pippen. I was surprised not to hear Ronnie's name on their radar.

I couldn't do much to disguise my appearance anymore, being that I was the underboss. It was from me having my face in every city and meeting the real heavy money makers that we were able to score and buy so many drugs from Hosea. Hosea was a better connect than Carlos and Felix.

I already knew that once we reached this status, the only thing more important than the money was our reputation. And I couldn't let Police Chief Atkins just take our money and think he could hide behind that badge.

Barry

Arriving at the DFW airport, I proceeded with caution and presumed to be as low key as possible. While retrieving my luggage, I was greeted by Yack, a Captain from the east side of Dallas who had come to pick me up. Although the news of my newfound son took me by surprise, Brandi eased my spirits by showing me pictures of Barry Junior before we departed. His snaggletooth smile made me feel as though there was more to life than what I'd thought. I wanted to be a father to my son as my dad was to me.

The players I had come up with in the game were actually using me when I thought about it. Everyone I thought I was helping out was just using my resources to their advantage as they took situations into their own hands. And now that someone tried to kill me, that was not how I wanted to be remembered by my son.

As Yack took my luggage and placed it inside the trunk, his BMW quietly pulled off into the traffic, but it wasn't long after we left the airport before we were pulled over and taken into custody. As fate would have it, this was just the first of several minor arrests from now through mid-November, where the police would come up with phony charges to harass me.

And every time, I dusted their charges off as if I had a dream team of lawyers to call on whenever I needed them. My criminal defense team of attorneys consisted of Kirk Warner from Dallas, a Jewish lawyer named Albert Capenski and Robert Stewart from Louisiana.

Sitting inside the investigation room, I was faced with several ATF Special Agents that gave me a fair warning of not to leave the city because I was under investigation and that my passport had been revoked. Not being the least bit intimidated, I yawned as he went on a rampage expressing how determined they were to take down my organization.

"We got fifty pounds of marijuana from a drop off kid in Memphis and $345,000 in small bills at a Money Mobb Mafia stash house in Miami. Not to mention one hundred and forty-seven kilos of cocaine in a downtown condo in New Jersey, but we're going to charge that to your buddies Des and Jr." He paused before another agent interceded with a smile.

"Don't forget to tell him about the drug house in Nevada we raided with over half a million dollars in cash saran wrapped underneath the bed. Or the seizure in Tulsa, Oklahoma where we found one hundred and eighty-eight kilos of cocaine still stamped with machine guns in the garage."

"It seems as though you gentlemen have been doing your homework." *Never let them see you sweat,* pops would tell me. "And since all you have is that, I would advise ya'll to get some tutoring after this session because you still don't have enough to amount to anything."

When we all entered the elevator one at a time, I could see the joyful expressions on Yack's and his soldier's face as they were surprised about their speedy release.

"Relax fellas. When your money is right, you can damn near look any charge in the face and walk out the same night."

Ronnie

When Barry and I met this evening, I knew he sensed the heat coming after us. The only question was when they'd actually come. All three of us were seeing less and less of one another nowadays. Agents were relentlessly taking pictures, sitting and waiting in their cars and tailing us through out the city. It got to the point where when we did actually meet up, it would be alongside a highway outside of town or sometimes in a airplane hanger at the airport. Donell never admitted to it, but he wasn't open for discussing exit routes outside the Mobb

"Wassup bro."

"Shit, niggas selling us out to the Feds every time I turn around. It's like these dudes look after themselves when they get around the police."

"Yeah I feel you bro." I said studying his actions before I continued.

"By the way B, I appreciate you sending me that Jewish lawyer, Capenski. He really got in them cops' shit for holding me up downtown."

"That's nothing bro. I'm here for you like I told you when you first got out."

"Well man, I hope you enjoyed your Fourth of July weekend because dudes down here were definitely firing off fireworks, ya feel me?"

"What the hell happened now?"

"Well… Long story short, JD went into the projects to do deliver a package and it was a setup. Cap and Benny were killed in the process too. Donell was pretty upset about you not being anywhere to be found. But I'm glad you were *out of sight out of mind* because the Feds were having a field day snapping pictures of all the Captains, Lieutenants and soldiers down with the Mobb."

"You gotta be fucking kidding me. I was just gone for one week." Barry said looking at the passing traffic while shaking his head in disbelief. I myself couldn't get the sight of Cap's sisters and brothers sobbing at his funeral out of my head. Filled with anger, I knew more than anything that going after my friends' killers wasn't what I should do, but I should get away from everything taking place before it was too late, or let alone me in a casket.

"Look man, we've been here a minute too long, we got to go. But you can't let this news take your head out the game."

"You're right Ronnie, we should leave here."

Through my rearview mirror, I watched my brother's Aston Martin Coupe merge into traffic without even signaling. I knew deep down inside that all the money and cars weren't worth my friend's life—let alone my brother's.

In between watching Barry and Donell come into this street life, and me being the only one left standing after my friends died, I drifted off thinking about Jason and how he felt at the end of the movie *New Jersey Drive*:

> "We were just trying to make our mark in the world, find something we could call our own, and if I've changed at all, it's only because I've seen too much. It's only because my life can't go back the way it was. Even if I wanted to, there's no going back."

Chapter 26

Conflict Of Interest

"These busta niggas don't know how much time they got left, better count every breathe . . . dumb move now you the one who gotta rest in peace . . ."   *JT Money—Anticipation Of Death*

Donell

"YEAH YEAH MAN, that nigga's done, we silenced that pig." Bodie said over the phone, with his adrenaline still at an all time high.

"Was it any people that saw you or what?"

"Kinda, sorta. Because it's noon, you got neighbors coming and going. You know what I mean?"

"Yeah yeah, I feel ya." I agreed staring into my colossal closet.

"But I had a mask on ya feel me? These white mothafuckas didn't see shit but the explosion and flames blasting from that dude's house."

"Yeah, well that's what happens when someone steals from the Mobb and don't think we're coming after they ass."

Bodie and the hit he had done was only part of the business to be handled today. I was getting ready to fly out to East St. Louis tonight and close a four million-dollar deal with Stanley and his new connect that he had already been buying drugs from.

When I walked out of my room, I couldn't help but admire the bubble curves and exotic features that Shannon's body had as she stood nude cooking breakfast.

"You want some cheese in your grits, Donnie?"

"Naw baby, they do that shit in Miami, us country boys in Texas only add sugar." I said smiling before going to turn on the plasma television.

Ronnie

Walking into my condominium I felt relieved to be getting out of this life, but depressed at the price I had to pay to finally realize it. I sometimes thought about the sad fact that my mother and father were both deceased. My best friends were dead and now the only two brothers I had left were caught up in the crossfire, like victims.

Barry once told me that he'd seen something in Christina that he hadn't seen in a lot of women. He recognized what type of woman she was by the way she respected me. He said she had the same aura as Brandi and that we both shouldn't make the same mistake—that I should keep a woman like her and let this life we live go.

As I had done that night he saved my life, I took his advice and took Christina with me to buy a townhouse on Gibbs Beach in Barbados. After all the nightmares I had, and crazy things I'd done, standing on that white sand beach facing the turquoise water made me feel as if I was in a commercial. It made me feel good to buy my first place and even better to be something my parents, friends and cellmates couldn't be: free and at peace.

Barry

From the back seat of my Rolls Royce Phantom, I was on a roll collecting money from contracts. At the same time, I was still frustrated by what had taken place earlier this week. Police Chief Atkins was killed and I knew that shit was definitely going to come back and haunt us. It would haunt us all the way downtown to the cold investigation rooms, to the stale-smelling courtrooms where they would try to pin that shit on the Mobb and me in particular.

I thought about Brandi and how much I confined in her to relieve my stress. I thought about how emotional I'd get when I would speak to my son, and how he would respond with such innocence in his voice. I may have contemplated on it before I went to Florida, but leaving the game behind was definitely my priority now.

By noon I had made the majority of stops, but I still had a few more pickups to make when it came over the radio for what seemed like the one hundred and forty-fifth time.

"There are still no witnesses that can come up with any leads as to who

is responsible for the murderous home invasion and bombing of Police Chief Atkins, who was survived by his wife and three kids. Authorities believe this to be in connection with the infamous Money Mobb Mafia. The task force also believes the Money Mobb Mafia has something to do with the killing of Federal undercover Agent Kyle Thomas and Detective Chaz Jacobs."

Exceedingly distressed, I couldn't wait to meet with Donell about what he had ordered before his flight left. I checked my Audimer watch for the time and eavesdropped on the incoming call my driver answered.

"Don B, we just took a hit for eight hundred grand in Miami." Terrel said, attaching the phone back to its console in the front seat while looking through the rearview mirror at me.

"FUCK! Gimme the details."

"They caught two hundred kilos of cocaine, seventy-five pounds of weed and thirty pounds of heroin in a sweep of three stash houses, along with four hundred grand."

I stared out the window as my first concern had to do with Kingston. He was my long time friend from A&T and he was definitely going to need a lawyer if he stood a chance at beating these new charges due to the fact that he had prior felony charges.

"You answer the phone saying number one as if that's your real name." Diana said with a smile, staring at Terrell as he drove.

Terrell was my youngest nephew on our dad's side of the family. His mother moved him down here from Virginia to keep him from getting into trouble, but what she didn't know was that we *were* trouble, and responsible for over twenty-eight homicide cases alone in Virginia and controlled sixty percent of the cocaine being bought and sold in the seven cities.

Diana found it humorous how I had my methods of communication set up, to say the least.

Nowadays, you had to go through several people before word got back to me about what happened. Kingston had to call number three, who was a mule in Arkansas. She would then accept the initial phone call and note the details and bond money to pass onto number two. Number two would then hire a lawyer and bail everyone involved out. Number two would then turn around and call number one who would relay all the information to me down to the T. Terrell would tally up all the bond monies, lawyer fees and minor expenses and tell me the total lump sum loss.

Arriving at a car garage in the business district downtown, I had to mentally gather myself.

"Wassup bro?" Donell said nonchalantly.

"Shit! The news, the media and all the other mothafuckas that you've woke up to what the hell we're doing down here."

"Man Barry, Chief Atkins had to get dealt with. He robbed us—he robbed the Mobb, so he *had* to get made an example of."

"Everyone knows he did it!"

"That shit is on Fox 4 News, Channel 11 News and bits and pieces are on CNN."

"Who the hell did you even get to *do* that crazy shit?"

"Oh don't worry Barry, I got Bodie, so it wasn't a trace left."

"Man, it's pictures everywhere of that pig's house in flames. His whole damn front door, kitchen windows, and even his minivan were burnt up." I said using my fingers to count the damages that occurred.

"Well, you know how he don't like the police."

"Aw hell, I can't tell because he damn sho brought the police to the Mobb, and now we're the *Infamous* Money Mob Mafia."

"Look man, how bout you just turn the empire over to me since this shit is becoming too much. I mean, I guess that shootout still got you shook. Niggas die every day B, you can't let some random niggas make you throw in the towel after all we've worked for." He said, staring into my eyes as if this was all he ever wanted.

"Okay, bro. You go do that deal with your boy Stanley and I'll tell Hosea tonight that you'll be the one running the show." I said, mentally exhausted from trying to understand my younger brother's way of thinking.

Watching Donell slowly stroll over to his convertible, I was taken back to see him behind the steering wheel of his Lamborghini Murcielago Roadster.

"Oh… You like? You know the new shit for the next year comes out in September… I got to keep my whip game proper."

Terrell drove out the opposite side of the parking garage while I thought about my brother and how he was so caught up with being on top that he didn't realize that we were on our way to retiring and being free at the same time.

Chapter 27

Lights, Camera Action

"... We keep hoes crunk like Trigga man, Fo'real it don't get no bigger man, don't trip, let's flip, getting' throwed on the flip, gettin blowed with the motherfuckin Jigga man..." Jay-Z ft. UGK—Big Pimpin

Donell

STANLEY AND I WERE more like brothers after all we'd been through. I thought back to how he was the first person to sell me my first eight-ball to how to cook cocaine. The Mobb had now made millions and he was still by my side.

As my plane landed at the Lambert St. Louis International Airport at 11:45 p.m., I had only one thing on my mind, and that was making more money. At first making deals for a quarter million dollars made me nervous because I had never seen that much money before, period, but then it went to half a million dollars every other day. And now that it was a million here and a million there, it was normal.

When Stanley met me at the baggage claim, I could see the expression of excitement all over his face. Every time we would close a deal for more than half a million dollars, he would go off into a speech about how we should be proud of ourselves for doing things in a major way and how I was the real Don in his eyes. Sometimes I felt he disliked my brother because he wanted us to be closer, but Stanley never gave me a reason to say something against him.

Even with big plans for tomorrow, we still had time to kill tonight and I was going to really put it down as a night to remember in the *Lou*.

"Yo Stan, what we're getting into tonight homie?"

"Man, you mean *who* we're getting into tonight?" He responded turning his head to me with a huge grin. Laughing at his freaky sense of humor, my eardrums were damn near busted as his Alpine sound system played *2 Live Crew's Greatest Hits'* "Bill So Horney."

At my three-story condo, Stanley waited in my living room on the first floor while I got dressed. Since we were going to a strip club, I wore two chains. One fourteen-carat gold panther link necklace and the second was my domed Omega necklace with a charm medallion that read *Money Mobb Mafia*. Both flooded with diamonds, I topped it off with a Master Pilot Joe Rodeo watch and matching bracelet. Heading out of my room, I grabbed two pinky rings with the matching studded earring and seventy thousand dollars in cash just before we left.

"Damn Donnie, you shining, ain't cha."

"Oh I'm leaving with half the club tonight bro."

When we finally pulled into the Pink Slip strip club parking lot, I was already high from smoking weed while driving there, and in the midst of following Stanley I called Danny D who gladly said he would come through while I was there.

The moment we entered the club, I was shown mad love from all the bouncers, soldiers and Captains. I saw a familiar look in all their faces. It was the same look that everyone had in their eyes when Barry spoke. I knew I had the respect I wanted when I seen how they all hung on my every last word. And when the strippers saw the owner and manager come from the back office to shake my hand, I told the bartender to get me the most expensive bottle in the house. A few minutes went by before she returned from the back with a bottle of L'Esprit de Courvoisier.

Seated inside the V.I.P booths, I grabbed a waitress and told her to bring us two of the finest women working tonight that wanted to get paid and roll out with some *made* niggas.

"Okay." She said with a smile bigger than Texas.

"Yeah I see ya'll niggas tipping, but I'm bout to change the weather in this bitch." I lit up another Swisher Sweet blunt while watching the waiter I spoke with earlier walk back to us with two of the baddest dancers on the floor. I then sent the first dancer to the DJ with a thousand dollars in her hand, and told her to tell him not to let the music stop. When she returned, DJ Squeeky went into a routine that had everybody jamming, dancing, and tipping like they had just got their tax returns.

"Oh yeah. The Mafia in this bitch! My nigga Donell in this bitch!"

"It's niggas out here that claim they getting money, but the Mobb showing ya'll that we *already been had* money!"

The more he played music, the more I threw one hundred dollar bills to make the dancers run wild as they grinded and gyrated their asses on my dick, making it harder. I'd already blown fifteen thousand dollars and tore the seal off my second $10,000 band when I seen Stanley smiling at the DJ.

"Shit don't stop cause a nigga get knocked!"

When the DJ began playing "Pimp Hard," "Boom Boom," "Don't Flex," and "Get It Crunk" by 8Ball & MJG, I noticed one dancer in particular eyeing me from across the room who I hadn't yet seen until just now. Her muscular and juicy thighs reminded me of a Clydesdale stallion the way her body was so toned. Stepping down from the V.I.P platform, I made my way through some soldiers to approach her before the DJ started back blasting the music.

"It's not polite to stare, so I figured since I'm a gentleman underneath all the glitz and glamour, I'd introduce myself, so we both can know who we're dealing with."

"Oh well, I'm Keke and I just seen you over there with that big ole entourage and I didn't know if I was welcomed."

"Baby if you're down to leave here with me and my boy right there-" I said turning around to point out Stanley in the midst of the crowd. "Then you're more than welcome to join our dynasty, courtesy on behalf of the fly and paid Bosses' Commission."

She then cracked a smile and blushed at what I said before saying, "Well I guess."

"Naw, Keke baby, you can't do any guessing or hesitating when you join our camp, ya dig? From now until tomorrow morning, every dancer leaving with us is down for whatever."

"I'm down, but can I bring my girlfriend Diamond out the dressing room first?"

"Sure."

Quickly walking to the back, she returned with a dancer that topped every one I'd seen up until now.

How many mo' bitches back there?

Starring trying not to act stunned, I observed her slowly walk out with her ass and breasts glistening as if she had applied baby oil on them before she voluntarily greeted me with a more than friendly hug.

I walked ahead of both of them to the V.I.P platform while the entourage of soldiers instantaneously parted, making an apparent and obvious pathway for them to follow behind me with ease.

"Ya'll niggas thought we was done. Shit, we was only taking a break!"

The DJ yelled with authority in his voice before going off into a mixture of songs by random artist such as UGK, Trick Daddy, and Pastor Troy. I stood over the two dancers, throwing stacks of fifty and hundred dollar bills that fell to the floor after sliding off their backsides when I seen Danny D walk in discreetly. I then told Stanley that I was going to holla at him real quick when I noticed the two of them nodding at each other with much familiarity.

"Wassup D?" I said as we walked inside the restroom to hear one another over the loud bass in the club.

"Shit, what's the deal Donell? I see you out here doing your thang, shutting the scene down like it's your homecoming."

"Aw, same ole shit, just a different day big homie. And you?"

"I'm bout to disappear dawg. A local police pig said it's a big time sting going to take place tomorrow."

"Oh yeah?"

"Did he mention anything about them hitting any of the Mobb stash houses?" I asked now with my curiosity at an all time high due to the fact that I was not only closing a deal for four million dollars, but it was with a dude I'd never even met before.

"Yo, check this Danny, I came across this dude named Pound. You heard of him moving dope around here? He's supposed to be someone heavy in the streets."

"Naw my nigga, that name doesn't ring a bell." He said with his hand rubbing against his chin as if he was still thinking.

"You for sho, D?"

"My nigga, I'm Danny D. If I don't know *you* then you ain't moving anything heavy, but you know what? Let me make a call."

When he got off the phone, Danny D told me that the person he just spoke with said they hadn't heard of him either. All the while, the person on the other end of the phone answered his question rather quickly and without hesitating. It was as if this supposed- to-be-big-time connect didn't exist. As we left the bathroom, the only thing on my mind was getting some information out of Stanley tomorrow morning.

As the last call for alcohol came and went, so did my interest for lap dances and smoking blunts with a hard-on. I had two strippers with me in the corner butt naked and they were more ready than ever to leave once I slid them both half an ecstasy pill.

"Donell baby, we about to go and get changed so we can leave out of

THE COMMISSION

here with you. We're riding with you to your place, right?" she said while putting her G-string swimsuit back on.

"Yea, ya'll gone ahead and do that." I said while admiring Keke's cocoa butter-colored skin. She was the thickest out the two with an ass that stuck out far enough to sit a drink on. She had deep alluring eyes along with an angelic baby face. Even though she told me she was 22, the younger of the two, she still could be a model with her photogenic smile. That's what caught my attention when I initially approached her across the room. Beside the fact that she had a chest that had to be a 36C with a small waist, it only made her ass seem larger than life, as it had to be a size 42.

If that bitch didn't get shots in her ass, then she definitely is going to take some from me tonight.

Her friend Diamond was the best looking woman in the club, with naturally long and curly hair all the down to her backside with well-toned thighs and a flat stomach. She was the tallest out of the two with no tattoos, which made her beauty that much more majestic as I remain mesmerized at her slanted eyes and flawless candy complexion.

After Stanley got into his coupe with a light skinned Dominican stripper, he followed me as I had Keke ride in Diamond's lap on the passenger side.

"Ya'll hold on tight now," I said as I started to switch gears, merging into traffic onto the freeway while listening to JT Money's *Playa Ass Shit*.

While I drove with the strippers riding beside me, they continued to sip the rest of my eight thousand dollar bottle of Courvoisier sharing the same cup. I casually glanced over and caught Diamond kissing on the back of Keke's neck. *It's going down,* I thought to myself as I exited the freeway and pulled into the garage. Half drunk, it wasn't that hard to put my thoughts off about this dude Pound that Danny D had never heard of, but when all this shit wore off, I'd be ready to address the fake with the real shit.

"Ohh Donell your place is nice," Diamond said with big eyes not hiding the fact that she had never been inside such a magnificent condo.

As I turned on the fireplace, I went to my weed stash in the closet and brought back a quarter pound of chronic for everyone to smoke on. Keke broke down the buds while sitting Indian style on my plush brown leather futon. Stanley then pulled me to the side telling me that he was going to use my guest room on the third floor to put his sex game down with the Dominican chick. That was fine by me.

Sitting with in-between the two with my arms stretched out, Keke laid her head in my lap, kissing my six pack, then my bellybutton all the way down until she pulled out my shaft to see how long and hard I was. She then licked on me first before taking me into her mouth. Up until now, I was only envisioning how good it would feel with her thick and plump lips on my dick. I leaned up only for Keke to pull my pants down, while at the same time fingering Diamond as Keke got on her knees to pull down the rest of my pants. Keke managed to pull my pants all the way off before separating my balls with her warm tongue as she began to lick and then suck on them one by one before licking my entire shaft. Taking her time, her hands were on my thighs as she rested her soft big breasts in between my legs.

Just as horny as Keke and I, Diamond played with her nipples underneath her shirt. I then took the blunt back into my mouth and leaned over to remove Diamond's shirt around the same time Keke began deep throating my dick, making me briefly close my eyes. Once I removed her shirt, Diamond took more sips of her drink as she stood to take off her panties. Standing facing me, Diamond placed her hand on Keke shoulder slowly bringing her head to a complete stop as it was going in an up and down motion. Diamond then looked at me.

"Daddy, I want to see what this Louis XV taste like on yo dick," while looking at my saliva covered dick as she waited for me to give her the *OK*. Keke got up and took off the rest of her clothes. *These bitches are crazy. Hoe this brown futon was imported from Italy not Ashley. You freaky bitch, this cost eight grand. Fuck it.*

"Sure."

As Diamond slowly got on her knees, one at a time and poured the liquor on my dick, she quickly raced to lick it up before it got a chance to run off me unto the futon. She then slowly jacked my dick off with her left hand and slurped it while stroking my shaft delicately, using her fingers. When Keke grew impatient from sipping liquor and smoking the last of the blunt, she put it down only to get on her knees behind Diamond and massage her butt cheeks before leaning back, using one hand to finger her vagina from the back while putting two fingers using her free hand in her ass as well.

Leaning forward from the futon, I used the inside of my forearm to pull the back of Diamonds' head toward my stomach so I could reach out and smack her ass with my right hand and palm her butt cheek with the left one. Her moaning when I smacked her luscious brown booty confirmed that was exactly what she wanted.

"Lick her ass. Tongue kiss her booty hole, Keke."

Diamond loved every bit of it as she moaned louder, and squeezed my dick all the while bobbing her head going up and down faster never missing a beat. When I reached into my pocket to spark up another blunt that I didn't use in the club, I started to grow impatient with oral sex.

"Let's change this up," I said as I lit the blunt and inhaled it deeply at the same time. "How bout ya'll taste one another on my rug right there," I said pointing at my oversized Canadian Black Bear Fur Carpet that I had shipped from Russia. "Its getting a little too crowded. We need more room."

After Keke scooted her butt backwards to the rug, Diamond got up and walked over to stand over her. Keke then laid on her back with her legs open and knees up while at the same time fingering herself to the point where I could see her juices when she took her fingers out. Watching, Diamond slowly got on her knees, then her stomach. Before she put her hands underneath Keke's legs to palm her ass as she buried her head in-between Keke's thighs. Keke began to moan and bit her lip in ecstasy from the feeling of getting her pussy eaten by another woman.

Quickly leaving the room for a condom, I was turned on even more when I returned to see Diamond's magnificently shaped caramel ass up in the air, her pussy dripping juices onto my fur carpet as she ate Keke out while Keke ran her hands through Diamond's hair. Not wasting any time, I kneeled down, palming Diamond's cheeks with one hand, when she moaned without lifting her head up. Glancing at Keke's eyes half open, I threw on my Trojan Magnum.

Bringing Diamond's ass back to me, I inserted my dickhead when she raised her head from in between Keke's thighs only to look back and watch me put it into her wet pussy. Focused on stroking her cat, I watched her pussy cream all over my condom.

"Damn daddy yo dick is hard," she said biting her bottom lip with her eyes closed, while using Keke's knees as leverage to throw her ass back. As Diamond threw her ass back, I matched it with a strong, hard and long stroke that I could tell she wasn't used to. Every time she threw it back, I grabbed hold of her ass cheeks and kept them spread while I brought her closer to me making her take all of me inside until her juices dripped on top of my balls.

"Aw shit," Diamond mumbled as I used my left hand to push her head down into Keke's perfectly shaved vagina. As her head went down, her ass came up, allowing me to go deeper until I rose into a squatting position, where I leaned forward into every stroke with my left elbow buried into her lower back.

"Dah…Donell—I'm fucking coming!" She yelled while panting with both of her palms stretched out, rubbing Keke's breast as her head was now lying across Keke's stomach with her knees locked together. Once Diamond's right thigh ceased shaking, her knees slowly parted and her pussy echoed a subtle noise that sounded like air escaping her womb while dripping juices.

With my dick still throbbing, I strapped another condom on before asking Keke, "You ready to get yours now baby?"

Chapter 28

The Sky Is falling . . . .

". . . Ain't no love for a buster, no fear for no coward, no respect for no slut and no money without power . . ."   Lil Wayne—Block Is Hot

Barry

"OK I SEE THEM. Do you see them T?"

"Yeah, I see them, in that blue car, right?" Terrell responded as he looked through the rearview mirror preparing to break in my Porsche Panamera Turbo.

"Okay, I want you to signal with your left blinker but get over into your right hand lane when it's clear on my side."

Continuing to maneuver and mislead the undercover cops who were following us, we dodged them through a series of turns and lane changing, ending with us getting on another freeway. We finally lost them as we made our way to Forth Worth, Texas.

I'd woken up early today because I was cashing out accounts all over the city preparing for my big break. I had already met with some investment brokers and cashed out millions of dollars worth of stocks and bonds.

They got all the angles figured out. You know what capitalism is? Getting fucked. I thought about all the millions of dollars that I had put into these banks only to lose hundreds of thousands of dollars once I withdrew it. Taxes, points, and fees was all bullshit the bankers used for all sorts of reasons.

"They won't stop coming for you until you're finished. You have to get away before you regret still being there." I remembered my pops telling me sounding more remorseful than informative.

After our last pick up, that brought me to seven point eight million dollars, and that's when I decided it was just too much money to be driving around in one car. After putting six million dollars in the trunk of Diana's'

Suburban, Terrell and I rode with the remainder in the trunk of my Porsche.

Contemplating an alternate place to meet up with Hosea to pay him some money on behalf of Donell, I thought to myself about how people in my situation always ended up either dead or in jail.

Thinking to myself, I realized that either I had to leave these streets and win or lose everything when they came for me.

I remembered when Terrel got wind that his so called country cousins in Texas were well connected, and respected in the drug game. He thought he'd hit the jackpot, but he didn't. I wasn't going to let him get involved with the Mobb because what he failed to realize was that this game is easy to get into, but there is no getting out of it.

"I just want to be a millionaire. I see Donell riding around here in Lamborghinis and you're riding around in a Rolls Royce Phantom wearing suits looking like the black John Gotti. I am willing to do whatever to get my own. Hell, I'll be your driver kinfolk. Everybody got to start somewhere."

And on that note, I already had the simplest job for him to do. Making him a driver, as well as my number one, was the closet to scot free he could be. With him being my number one, I could keep a watchful eye on him and he wouldn't get his hands dirty. Hell, he was only nineteen.

I remember when my moms and I went to pick him up from the airport. On the way to the airport, she confronted me about knowing the truth as to who I really was, let alone how much of an unvarying reminder I was to her of my father. She walked up to me, held my face in the palm of her hands and just started into my eyes, saying how she didn't want to lose her whole family.

I visited my pops more and more, especially when Uncle Billy was indicted on money laundering and conspiracy charges and they always went the same way:

"You're getting too big son. I know you hear that voice in the back of your head talking to you. And I hope you listen to it, before you round up regretting that you didn't," my pops said staring into my eyes as if he knew exactly what I was going through. On my last visit, his eyes met mine, leaving me with an eerie feeling, as if I was him and my son was the one on the other side of the glass.

Today was halfway over, and I hadn't heard from Donell yet. Although it was my birthday today, I still wanted to check on him to see how he was, not because he hadn't called me.

I spoke with Brandi earlier this morning as we only talked about one thing, me getting the hell *out of dodge*. Our minds we made up on what had to be done, the next biggest issue was the timing to get everything shipped and mailed off. Nowadays we only discussed where to get all the furniture for the beach house, since Brandi had already moved her and Junior's belongings into the house.

Now the only thing that was missing was myself, the man of the house. I realized that the longer I stayed in the game, there were three things promised to me; betrayal, deceit and lies: there was no longer loyalty.

"What the fuck!"

"Man, I used my fucking blinkers, and I got the car in cruise control doing the speed limit. I don't know what the hell they're pulling us over for."

"Just be cool nephew."

After what seemed like an endless amount of questioning, the U.S. Marshalls asked us to get out of the car and stand alongside it. It was then when two unmarked squad cars pulled up, with three DEA agents in each, to assist the U.S. Marshalls.

After a thorough and swift search, they found exactly what they were looking for underneath a blanket and a stack of Sunday newspapers. In all big bills, nothing smaller than a twenty, in Louis Vuitton duffle bags was the $1.8 million dollars from this morning.

I looked to my nephew, then to the passing traffic alongside the service road before being shoved into the back of the unmarked squad car.

"We'll be out by tomorrow afternoon nephew, this is nothing." I said as I sat back in the squad car, thinking about spending my Sunday night birthday in the four star accommodations of the county jail.

Detective Johnson

"Alright guys, you did a good job." I said through the handheld radio as we followed behind Barry's Porsche leading the U.S. Marshalls directly to where he was.

"Now I'm going to need ya'll to take pictures of the money once we count and check it into the office."

"He has got to be one of the most tedious mothafuckas I have ever investigated. If only we could have gotten a tail on him earlier, we could have caught him with more money." Logan said in a depressed tone. Logan knew that when Cap, JD and Benny died, that was the beginning of the end.

"I'm surprised they haven't scattered like roaches with their muscle being gone."

"We got them Logan. I got them right where I want them."

"Oh yeah, just like Mike Millan had Barry's father? Or just like Jacobs thought he had Donell's goons fooled?"

"You can't think for one minute that you're in still waters. Remember that the calm comes before the storm Johnson."

"Don't get relaxed, don't allow yourself to be put into a predicament that isn't worth your life."

Things were getting crazier since we were systematically taking apart the Money Mobb Mafia organization, one Boss and one city at a time.

The closer we got to taking their organization down, the more anxious I grew to make it all happen. I was tired of not knowing whether or not Barry had me made. Tired of going to therapy, growing dependent on sleep-inducing drugs. I was frustrated with living on the edge, having to murder hustlers to keep my cover from being blown. The only thing that made me pursue this investigation every morning was remembering the fact that it was up to me to bring my partners who had lost their lives true justice.

Chapter 29

Blood Thicker Than Water . . . .

". . . Yo Money listen, I'm going to tell you something. If he's not who you say he is, I'm going to kill'em, then I'm going to kill you . . . ."
                                                          Wesley Snipes-New Jack City

Donell

WHEN I WOKE up the next day, I could barely feel my face after all the drinking, smoking and ecstasy I took last night. I sat up in bed and looked to my left to see Keke with her face buried in the pillow. I checked my beeper before my phone and seen that Barry had called me twice and beeped me once. Although it was well past morning, I still hadn't received a phone call from Stanley as to when exactly the deal was to go through. I made a mental note to call him when I smelled some pancakes and bacon being cooked.

These hoes done stayed the night, I thought as I washed my face and brushed my teeth before heading downstairs to check on Diamond. Once I got to the bottom of the stairs, she looked as if she had been awake for a while. She was wearing a totally different outfit, looking better today than she had the night before. She wore dark see-through purple boy shorts and a matching bra that had *Victoria's Secret* written all over it.

"Good morning Donnie," she said, turning from the stove with a nonstick skillet in her hand and emptying the pancakes onto a second plate.

"What's happening? I see you cooked a brotha breakfast."

"Well you're vey welcome Donell." She said smiling as she walked by me brushing her booty against my semi-hard dick on her way headed to the living room, where she had already started the movie *The Best Man*.

"When I start eating this, I'm not leaving any for Keke."

"Oh don't worry about her. That girl sleeps 'til two, three o'clock."

As I sat there and ate, I rolled me another blunt to smoke for when I got out the shower. In the midst of me sitting there, I still was surprised by all the pictures that Rhonda had put together and put around my place. She had pictures of me playing college ball, pictures of Barry and me at the club, and pictures of me gambling at the Bally's Belle of Orleans casino. Then my thoughts turned to this mystery hustler.

Why the fuck hasn't anyone heard of him?

Sure we had some stash houses and a few soldiers caught up, but because I wasn't included in Barry's number man system, I was left out the loop of the details when it came to certain matters.

When I called Stanley, I could tell that he was well awoke and coherent.

"Wassup Donnie."

"Shit. You tell me my nigga, when we're going to start the party?"

"We're still on my nigga, plan A, number one." he said in code, knowing already what I was calling for.

"Oh, okay then. I want you and me to meet up at number two first."

Stanley and I would talk in codes when we had to use a phone because we talked about everything in person. Whenever we did a deal period, when money would be involved, we would refer to Plan A. Plan B simply meant it's not going to happen anymore. Now the original spot where the exchange was supposed to take place at was referred to as number one. Now, number two was an alternate spot, usually secluded on the other side of town, where we would go if things went wrong.

Once I hopped into the shower, I relaxed under the warm water behind the fogged glass doors. *I hope my brother isn't that mad at me because I missed his call. Hell, I knew it was his birthday yesterday. I didn't forget . . . I just got caught up,* I thought to myself before being interrupted when I heard the shower door squeak open.

"Aw, I'm sorry Donell." Keke said with only one foot in the shower stopping herself from getting in all the way. "I thought you were Diamond."

"Oh you're cool. I'm almost finished." I said trying to act as if she didn't just startle the shit out of me. *Freaky ass bitches. I'm going to have to save their numbers in my phone, so next time I can get'em and hit'em both in the shower.*

Putting my head underneath the showerhead stream of warm water, she had another thing coming thinking she could join me in the shower and we'd probably end up fucking. *It's money over everything.*

Once I got out and began getting dressed, I thought more about this suppose-to-be big sting taking place today that Danny D told me of last night.

I then called my Lieutenants and told them in codes to shut down all the operations immediately and put everything up, starting with the cash first, until they got a call from me or Barry giving them the green light to get things going again.

Once I was done getting dressed, I stopped by my jewelry box to grab and put on some *bling* before I headed downstairs. When I did so, I heard the melodies of Tony Toni Tone's "Whatever You Want" playing from my living room. Once I made it down, I stood in the kitchen and watched Diamond roll a blunt out of what was left from the chronic as Keke sat besides her doing what seemed like schoolwork.

Grabbing my keys to my Benz caught Diamond's attention as she looked up before putting the weed down and walking in my direction toward the kitchen.

"How much is it for an ounce of that 'dro you got?" she said, standing beside me while going inside her white leather Jimmy Choo purse as if she was looking for some money.

"Aw, naw baby, that's not 'dro we've been smoking. That there is chronic."

"Well how much can I get with two hundred dollars?"

"I couldn't tell you honestly. All I buy is pounds." I said staring into her eyes. Leaning up against the island counter top, all I remember thinking was-

If she only knew how big I was, she'd feel stupid for offering me two hundred dollars.

"I'll bring us some *kush* back baby, it's nothing." I said as I tapped her on her ass and headed out the front door.

When I pulled up into the parking lot of the Ritz-Carlton, I proceeded straight to room one-eight-seven. After knocking on the door, I reached and felt for my waist where I had my new chrome nine-millimeter pistol with a red laser light. I had bought it in California when the Mobb went to the Cash Money Brothers concert, and every time I was in St. Louis, I would leave it behind. But this time I was going to carry it around the whole day, up until I drove back to Dallas so I wouldn't forget it.

When Stanley opened the door and walked back to the bed, I saw two large sized black Prada duffle bags. And the only sound that could be heard

in the mid-sized room was the beep that went off periodically as he counted the money using three money machines.

"Wassup homie, I see you still letting bitches stay the night at your place." he said as he turned to face the money counter before sitting down. "You got to be careful bro, these bitches out in the Lou will try to catch you slipping while you sleeping."

"Yeah man whatever… I want you to tell me some more about this Pound nigga," I said sitting in the chair opposite of him, helping him neatly fold the money.

"Shit, he's just another real ass nigga that been holding it down in the Lou," he said, adding money to the already-full machine before pushing the start button. "You know, like whenever players can't get you, me or Danny D—he be right there at the door. He sells coke, weed, heroin, you name it."

"I'm saying though, Danny D been down with us for years and he hadn't never heard of this dude that claims he from here. If this dude is making all this money and connected to the point where he can put up four million dollars worth of drugs, then more than one person would vouch for him." I said, realizing that none of this was making sense to me.

"Look, Donnie. Do Barry question you when you come with a customer that want a shitload of weight? Hell naw! Do you go behind his back and check a nigga's street cred? Hell no again! That's cause ya'll trust each other." Stanley halfway stuttered through his speech while he went from standing in one position facing me, to moving to the bags to put the money inside.

"*Nigga you ain't my brother, you're my friend. You can never be my fucking brother. No matter how many times we fight and fall out, he's still my damn brother.*"

"Yo my nigga."

"I ain't saying I don't trust you, I'm just saying—"

"Naw my nigga. What are you saying exactly?" He said with an attitude as he stuttered some more causing me to think back on what my pops used to tell Barry and I when we were kids: *"A man who stutters is lying or has something to hide."*

"We got to trust one another, the same way you and Barry trust one another. How else are we going to run this empire we starting? My nigga, this is the score that's going to take us to that Tony Montana level dawg. You got to be all the way with me on this or not at all."

"Our empire? Nigga what the fuck you mean *our* empire?" I said as I slowly rose to my feet, all the while withdrawing my pistol while he had his back to me zipping up the bags.

"Nigga you're already *in* an empire. Nigga, me and my brother built a fucking empire from the ground up. We ain't starting another empire off no deal. I'm not with that. You think cause we're best friends that makes us brothers? Hell naw! I got only one brother and you can't be him," I ended, facing him with a cold stare as I now raised my gun at him sideways with the laser beam pointing in-between his eyes.

"Man what da fuck you doin'? You think I want to be that dude on the sideline forever? I been fucking with ya'll since ya'll started and I ain't even met neither one of ya'll connects. And if ya'll don't let me buy from ya'll's connect, then I'll get my own, but no more side line shit."

"That niggas' a fucking FED." I said, looking at him in his eyes. "You been down so long, you think you can bite the hands that feeds you, huh?"

"Donell. You're my best friend man. Me and you can do this," Stanley said standing still as his face made a drastic change to match his attitude all of a sudden.

Taking a step back, I fired off a single round that went out the back of his head as the bullet broke the glass going out the window.

Yeah we were best friends, but I'm my brother's keeper before anything else.

I then went about wiping down everything I touched, and picked up the duffle bags before leaving the room. In a trance, driving down the service road, I got onto the freeway and took I-64E to Louisville on my way to the house I had bought in an upscale community called Bella Meade, just outside of Franklin, Tennessee.

I'll go back and fuck with them bitches on another date, I thought while listening to C-Murder's *On My Enemies* before I called Wayne to tell him that I was going to need a stash spot while I stayed at my house in Bella Meade.

Chapter 30

Teflon Don

"... the game done changed, its not the same, the lost don be my name cause I'm true to the game..."   Master P—Streets Keep Me Rollin'

Brandi

*T*IME IS JUST *flying by and I'm not even sure if I'm going to have this place ready in time before Barry gets here for Christmas.*

"Boy, you better put your toys up and stop leaving them on the floor. You hear me?" I said, picking Junior's toy truck up off the floor and thinking about how much my life had changed since I left Baca Raton. I've been out here in Costa Rica for about three months now. Every since Barry said that he was serious about changing his lifestyle to start a family, my heart went from being on standby to having a pulse that beat twice as fast. This man was everything I ever wanted, and besides, he was the father to my child.

I'd been on cloud nine every since Barry enthusiactically accepted the fact that we had a son and now all I could think about was how Barry had been doing everything he said he would after that night. Everyday, I was just patiently waiting for our relationship to pick up where it left off.

Although it had been three long years, it was all behind me now as I looked toward the future of us being a family more and more. Since I've been here, my parents said I was crazy for leaving a six-figure job. Along with my friends, who said I was acting foolish for leaving a stable life to be with a Mob Boss.

"You know them niggas never survive in the movies girl. All you're doing is dreaming and you need to wake up before you get yourself hurt again."

I paid them all no mind as they didn't know how I had a void fulfilled in my heart that made my dreams come true at the same time. I saw love all over me.

"Barry Brad McCoy Jr! If you don't get your butt in this kitchen and put your plate up, I'm going to whip you. And I mean right now!"

"But mommy, I see daddy."

"What? Your dad is in Dallas," I said, walking into the living room where he stood two feet from the big screen television. I grabbed Barry Jr. by his shoulder and brought him closer to me while watching the CNN news.

"Barry don't do this to me again. Just come home to me please."

"... *Today is Monday December 12, 2000 and Barry Brad McCoy has just posted a record bail bond of four million dollars. The prosecutors referred to him as the Money Mobb Mafia Boss and Drug Lord having direct ties to the Miami Kingpin, Kingston Johnson as well as Carlos and Felix Hernandez, who have already been indicted on related charges and are now awaiting trail. The District Attorney accused Mr. Barry McCoy as being the Godfather of the underworld as he was not only apprehended with $1.8 million in cash but, an arsenal of machine guns and fully automatic assault rifles within his 2001 Porsche Panamera. Prosecutors say they were flabbergasted when the judge spoke of Mr. McCoy's Piaget diamond studded watch worth well over one hundred and forty-five thousand dollars...*"

Standing there in shock, I couldn't imagine the kindhearted Barry I grew to love in college as a high profile notorious criminal figure. I always felt that Barry had close ties to the wrong crowd and his willingness to help his friends would bring him down. And now I worried about his future and most importantly *our* future.

"... *Mr. McCoy was very respectful in the courtroom this morning as he was represented by two criminal defense attorneys. Attorneys Albert Capenski and Robert Stewart are very much known and popular amongst high profile cases.*"

The anchor woman went on to give Barry's lawyer a chance to make a statement to the public.

"*Our client Mr. Barry McCoy is a genuine businessman and has notable professional references that can vouch for him in a court of law. Instead of the police and federal law enforcement task force taking shots at my client to destroy his grand reputation, they should apply those same efforts into protecting him from evil.*"

The anchor ended as she stood in front of the crowded pavement filled with community activists that were both for and against Barry going to jail, "*As Mr. Barry McCoy left the courthouse today, he was referred to as the Teflon Don...*"

Ronnie

"Yo man, I'm in position. I cashed your check too."

Barry made a lot of phone calls after being booked and fingerprinted yesterday. While waiting for his lawyers to bond him out, he had me calling people on three way to collect his money.

Just as much as I knew Barry was up to something, so was I myself. I had cleaned out all my stash spots. *I'm never coming back,* I thought to myself while checking my rearview and side mirrors before answering my phone.

"Wassup?"

"Yo dawg. This Donnie, I'm out of town."

"Niggas got wet the other day, and I'm sending you two men in a box to the spot." Whenever one of us was referring to a million dollars, we would say "men." And so I knew he was sending two million dollars in a box to our stash house.

"Okay. I got you." I said hanging up the phone while waiting for Barry.

Barry

After fourteen long hours in that small, dirty and smelly cell, I was finally out of there.

I'm not ever going back there, I thought to myself as we drove into the car garage where Ronnie waited for us. My plan was to have Ronnie drive Diana, Terrell and myself to the airport after we switched cars where I secretly planned to go to New York and fly a private jet to Costa Rica.

Thinking back to when my lawyers came to bail me out, they wasted no time informing me of the countless charges that the Feds had against me. After hearing everything they had on me, I knew I didn't stand a chance.

The list went on and on, all the way leading up to a four hundred and fifty page- eleven count indictment. The indictment consisted of wire-tapped conversations, premeditated murder cases and capital punishment cases, along with all the routine activities that came from continuing a criminal enterprise with RICO violations.

I figured it wasn't no time like free time. Even though I had a little over two million dollars all together in containment fees for my attorneys, once I was released I definitely planned to turn into a ghost.

Once we all got into Ronnie's SUV, I thought about how I wouldn't be seeing Donell or Ronnie again for a long time. We all came into this game with our future mapped out and now we all feared for tomorrow because it wasn't promised.

Chapter 31

When The Smoke Clears . . .

"See, the thing about the game is . . . The shit don't stop. You could be hurting, it don't matter. Business still roll up on ya . . ."

Ace—Paid in full

Donell

"RIDING THROUGH THE hood with my homies getting smoked out . . ." Listening to Three Six Mafia made me reminisce about all I had seen in the game, from the moment I dived into it head first fresh off the basketball court to when it started getting good, all the way until it started going bad. *I got to shake this shit off and bounce the fuck back* I said under my breath while sitting in the passenger side of Danny D's Impala. In the midst of being in Tennessee, I coincidently ran into Danny while driving through the north side of Memphis looking for something to smoke on.

It only took a few days, and now I knew major players in the city on a first name basis. With Danny D's help and my street knowledge, I had already made a hundred thousand dollars just from selling coke and weed. I took it upon myself to go down to New Orleans and score a million out of the four million dollars worth of drugs from Hosea. I already knew that Hosea was in a vulnerable position. He not only had the Mobbs' whole re-up, but after seeing my brother on the CNN news, he probably figured that we all would fall off and become history. But I had even bigger plans, I had plans to make Money Mobb Mafia the richest black brothers in history. In between selling dugs and shopping, I found myself getting super high or just sitting in my indoor pool getting drunk by myself.

How could I trust anyone anymore? With the money I made, it made everyone close to me suspect. Deep down inside, I never knew that me wanting to make something of myself would drive others away, I just hate that my brother had to be one of them. It wasn't no use in talking to him anymore because our mentality had grown soo far apart.

Nowadays, I was swamped with running the operations from every aspect… I mean I was the only top dawg left, besides Danny. When I found out that players in Memphis had no steady connect when it came to scoring drugs, I made a name for myself by having the lowest price in town at fifteen grand a kilo.

Hearing my beeper go off, I checked and noticed that I had four missed calls from Ronnie.

I figured ole *Calvin Marshall* was staying *low key* with the heat everywhere was catching. After putting two and two together from my undercover informant, and my own knowledge, I figured out Ronnie's game. Ronnie was going out of the city and state wearing wigs to disguise himself, giving everyone who didn't know him a alias name of Calvin Marshall. I had to tip my hat to him because with the way players were name-dropping today, it was only a matter of time before they drop my real name if they hadn't done it already.

Ronnie

"Wassup Mr. Johnson? How have things been going up at the Recreation center?"

"Aw, well you know how things are going, Ronnie." He said lifting the heavy brown bag of groceries to put them into the trunk of his truck. "The city is taking their time coming up with the money to fund these kids' little league teams, just like they took their time coming up with the funds for Paul Quinn College sports. And you know what happened to all *those* athletes," he said hinting that he was well aware of what Donell did once he stopped playing basketball. "They all got off into the wrong thing, them streets. Either smoking or selling drugs, you know."

Aside from managing my block parties, Mr. Johnson mentored teenagers.

"Wassup, Junior," I said acknowledging Mr. Johnson's oldest son who walked out the store with some Lays chips and soda.

"Boy don't you understand every time you buy something, you got to buy something for your little brother," Mr. Johnson told his oldest son as we observed him walk back into the liquor store.

While we stood in the parking lot of the Food Store in the shopping center, pedestrians came and went as I watched Mr. Johnson open his door about to get in.

"Yo, Mr. Johnson, that money will be there, don't even stress on it. As a matter of fact, I'll pay for it."

"You're going to do what?"

Placing my hand on Mr. Johnson's shoulder, I repeated to him that I was going to pay before glancing into traffic. At that moment I noticed some guys approaching the liquor store.

"I said I'm go—" I said before I felt fire strike my body and travel into my rib cage.

PAT PAT PAT!

Peeking through my eyelids, I watched the gunman gun down Mr. Johnson. I recognized the youngster from the crowd in the nightclub parking lot.

Lil C told me about this niggas, but I didn't listen. Now look at me, I remembered watching Mr. Johnson fell to the ground.

Now with my eyes all the way open, I stared at the young black dude holding the pistol doing and all the firing. I saw that he was the only one of the three who crossed the street who didn't have a mask on.

"You're a bad motherfucker," I mumbled, staring into his cold eyes before I felt two more shots pierce my chest as well as one in my stomach. I always wondered how I would die. I thought to myself as I laid there in my own blood, as I had always known that one day everything I had done wrong would catch up with me.

When I felt my body being moved around, I shouted in pain. I then heard people yelling and car horns ringing as I barely opened my eyes to see the shooter get into his getaway car just as quickly as it all happened. So many images flashed in my mind as if I was watching a moving on fast forward mode.

I thought back to the last look into my father's eyes, to the glare in my mom's eyes when she awoke from her high. I remembered the first dude I ever killed as well and my brother Barry when he was waiting outside the jail in Beaumont. I remembered all my close friends I grew to love, only to lose them to the life I chose to live.

Don't let a nigga kill you, I remembered telling my friends, and now look at me. Riding in the back seat, I bounced up and down as we ran red lights, only slowing down to go over speed bumps. The heat from the bullets made me sleepy as I stared out the window watching us speed by all the buildings, the trees and white clouds.

Detective Johnson

"I can't fucking believe this shit. I risked my life and damn near got killed three times only to lose this slick mothafucker. Shit, I should have known that he would have crossed me."

I should have known he was going to run off into the wind like Tim Robbins from *Shawshank Redemption.*

"We're going to raid Donell at his house tomorrow with the ATF and U.S. Marshalls," Logan said walking by my desk.

I knew he pretty pissed my most recent report of Barry sliding underneath my surveillance team. I knew that as smart as he was, he wasn't going to call anyone who he dealt with because everything he'd built had collapsed on him.

"Okay, I'll keep my phone on me in the meantime and double check some references I made in the field on Barry's whereabouts."

"Don't worry. They always slip up, and that's when we're going to catch him," Logan said, not breaking a stride as he walked to his corner office. Logan had years of experience and was known to propel the careers of his subordinates who helped build the case, and here I was shit out of luck. I was just too damn close to being where I intended to stop thinking of ways to find Barry now.

Chapter 32

Heavy Is The Head That Wears The Crown . . .

"Somebody pulling me close to the ground. I can sense, but I can't see. I ain't panicked, I been here before . . . My heart, it don't ever quit. I ain't ready to check out . . ."   Al Pacino—Calito's Way

Barry

"AW SHIT...NOW *THIS* is what it's all about," I said into my cell phone with Brandi on the other end as I plopped down on the king-sized bed inside the Presidential Suite. She was still worked up from seeing me on the news. "It's a surprise when I'll be there, you just have our house ready. I'm going to be there before Christmas Eve though so we all can open up one present."

The Towers at the Waldoff Historian truly lived up to its legacy. Since I was a teenager, after seeing this hotel in the movie *Coming to America*, I said I wanted to stay at the very top.

"*Well I'm going to stay in Trump Towers. Way at the top,*" I remember Donell saying when I first mentioned it. He was always in competition with me. It was him always wanting to be better than me that made me realize that I needed to stay on top of my game. But nowadays he wanted to race me down a dead-end street.

There's more to life to getting a shot, than just hitting that jumper, I remember Tupac telling Duane Martin in the movie *Above The Rim*. While in the shower, I thought about all the things I'd done and place I'd went since we all had been there. Terrell, Diana and myself blew money without a care in the world as we shopped at every designer label maker on Fifth Avenue not to mention Bergdorf Goodman.

Thinking about how Donell had been doing, I did wonder where Ronnie decided to go off to. I remember him whispering that he was leaving and this was the last time we'd see each other.

As I was about to walk out my room to the lobby on my way to the train station, I heard a knock on the door. To my surprise, staring out the peephole, I seen it was Diana wearing an overcoat. Opening the door just enough for her to step in, I stuck my head out the room to see if anyone was watching the room.

"Barry my water isn't getting hot enough in my room, so I wanted to come take a shower in your bathroom," she said removing her overcoat revealing her flawless angelic curvy figure.

Even though Diana and I only sexed a few times throughout the entire time of us knowing one another, I seen it as more so a convenient coincidence. I knew from being with prior women to never mix business with pleasure.

If you freak'em, you got to leave'em. I thought to myself as I contemplated on commenting on how much she had blossomed since I first met her when she graduated from Howard University. Diana was a good girl with a thing for bad guys. She may have had a chance at getting with me when I first started making money in college, but now that I was making millions, her and her feelings had no choice but to take the backseat.

Diana's jet black and silky brown hair highlights were still damp as water made her honey skin glisten like oil.

"You can join baby. I see you're dressed, but I wouldn't mind a little company."

In-between seeing her silhouette and contemplating her invite, my cell phone started ringing.

"Hello."

"Wassup, little bro," I said, realizing it was Donell calling me from a 901 number.

"Yo Barry, Ronnie was out on the Southside and got caught slipping," Donell said in a hasty tone. "I got a call from Lil C and he said it looked like it was a hit. They knocked Mr. J off in the process."

"Word, I'm there," I said in a no-nonsense tone. Throwing on my skull cap, I didn't think as to what I should do next, but knew I needed to hurriedly get a cab to the JFK airport.

"I'm running downstairs Diana, I'll be right back."

When my cab pulled up to Penn Station, I caught the LIRR train to the LIRR's Jamaica hub. While there, I couldn't help but notice how grimy the alleys were and the size of the rats that were in the subways. Using my Metrocard, I then took the LIRR/Airtran and arrived at the JFK airport just in time to catch the last flight leaving to Dallas.

Special Agent Logan and Undercover Agent Johnson

"Any leads?" Special Agent Logan asked Johnson in a thrilled tone as if he was expecting good news.

"Nope, nothing at all."

"What? How could you be empty handed when we've been doing all this surveillance? We got to find Barry," Logan said frustrated. "Just because we know where his brother Donell is, doesn't change the fact that we need Barry as well."

"How did your guys lose him again?"

"Once they went inside the garage, they must have switched cars because my field agents said their solider was driving alone after he left the parking garage. I mean my guys were right there and we still couldn't tell where he went."

"Well, keep your eyes open."

"Alright sir."

While Logan could safely go home, I knew I couldn't. With Barry nowhere to be found, and Calvin Marshal still at large, I was too paranoid not to think that he hadn't made me. I managed to stop drinking, but with my nerves still on edge, I knew I had to relax so I could think clearly about how I could find him.

All alone in the office, my computer screen lit my cubicle as I had visions of seeing my partners lose their lives. Going through a midlife crisis at twenty-six years old, I checked my hidden stash of Valium only to find it missing. Rapidly pulling out my desk drawers, I found my whole stash was cleaned out.

Fuck my life! This is the wrong time for this shit to be happening. The chirping of my beeper disturbed my thoughts as I checked it.

Barry

After a three-hour flight, I was back in Dallas. From the backseat of Ole School's cab, I called to Wayne have make me a fake passport with the fake pictures that he already had of me, as well as book me a private flight to Costa Rico.

"Don B, fam. Shit been crazy fam, it's crazy out here yo. You and your brother Donell are smart for leaving this place. Some fella out here was shot and killed in the grocery store parking lot not long ago. I'm not sure who he was, but they said he was someone big. I think they said that dude's name is Calvin, Calvin something. I can't remember. Some grocery store employees claim they seen the whole thing take place, and say it was more like a hit.

"Damn," I said, hoping Ole School was exaggerating. "I hope he pulls through," I added while directing Ole School into the hospital parking lot. When Ole School went inside to check the coast, I stayed seated inside the cab thinking about how I had to get him out of this mess. Thinking back on the incident with Maserati Rick, I knew anybody could walk in and finish my brother off and I couldn't live with that on my conscience. Singing "It's Like That" by Run DMC, Ole School returned with a smile on his face.

"Yo fam, you got the green light," He said walking around the trunk of the cab to where I was being seated.

"I searched the place pretty good and there wasn't any security."

Oh yeah. Well here, Ole School, take this." Sticking my hand outside the window, I handed him two grand- one thousand for my ride, and one thousand for him to pick Ronnie up once he was released.

"Now take this and drive me up to the hospital, I'm going to get out at the curb."

Special Agent Logan

"Yeah. I got your ass now." I said aloud staring through my binoculars from across the street on the third floor of a public parking garage.

I knew it was only a matter of time before Johnson started taking medication while working the case. And I just knew it would affect his thought process sooner or later. And with that being said, I picked up the slack double checking Johnsons' progress reports. Studying Barry's every move, I knew this latest shooting had to be in some way connected to the Mobb. And goddammit, I couldn't have been more right.

I've been working these cases for years now, and Ronnie McCoy couldn't pull the wool over my eyes by deceiving me into thinking that it was Calvin Marshall responsible for all these unsolved murders. Underneath the pile of indictment papers, in between the black and white facts, my gut told me it was him.

"I knew our boy ole Barry would show up. I'm going to take this motherfucker down right here, right now," I said raising my walkie-talkie at the same time.

"I want everybody to stand easy on station."

Barry

Standing in the patient room, I was taken back by all the different machines, tubes and monitors. I was filled with emotion. With his shirt off, gauzes covered his chest as the machine breathed for him.

"He's in pretty bad condition, but he does have a chance of pulling through. It's going to take some serious recovery time, not to mention therapy," The nurse said as she glanced at me while checking his blood pressure levels then noting the results on her clipboard.

"Look, um…"

"It's Nurse Jenkins, my name is Nurse Jenkins."

"Nurse Jenkins, how can we go about getting my brother to a private physician? He already has insurance."

"Yes, he does… And that's very possible, but lets not forget that there service is extremely expensive." With an early new years tax return, within two hours, Nurse Jenkins, Ronnie and I were in the back of an ambulance preparing to leave Parkland. Trying to look away and keep a vague face, I could barely stand the sight of seeing Ronnie stretched out with bullet wounds left as open scars to heal over time.

"He hasn't opened his eyes since he arrived at the hospital last night," she said as the paramedics strapped him down to their bed. As a shock to everybody, Ronnie's phone began vibrating. I then retrieved and answered it.

"Yeah. No, I mean not exactly."

Undecided as to how much to say over the phone, I decided to cut the conversation with Christina short after I took her address down in codes. Blinded by the glare of silent sirens flashing, I slowly rose out my seat surprised to see the police cars that swarmed the streets. Uniformed officers who were on foot persistently passing information amongst one another inspecting every car in traffic in search of someone comparing the people they seen with pictures they all carried.

Special Agent Logan

If he thinks he's going to sneak out of here in the back of someone else's car, then he's got another think coming.

"Lets take our time when we go to approach that ambulance, we don't know if Barry is in there." Logan said directing the field supervisor while he accepted a phone call.

"Hey, Logan call off your guys right now!"

"What the hell do you mean? We're on the verge of something big here."

"We're going to meet. I can do this Logan."

"You've done enough. I found your stash and I know all about you abusing your refill policy on behalf of the Bureau."

"Listen to me! What you're doing now is redundant plus it's too risky with these pedestrians and everybody in jeopardy in case he is armed."

Highly upset, Logan knew that it would be better to wait than to put innocent people's lives at stake.

"You better be right on this one, Johnson. We're still going to take his brother down tonight."

Barry

Riding alongside Ronnie on our way to the hospital, he opened his eyes up briefly, long enough to squeeze my hand.

Man, I hope you don't die.

Once Ronnie was safely receiving medial attention, I left in pursuit of going to our stash house not far from the hospital. Second guessing myself ever second that went by, I had this strange feeling as if any minute someone was going to kick in the doors or run out from inside a closet and arrest me.

"This shit isn't worth getting caught."

I hoped that I wasn't being watched. I knew with Donell in Memphis and myself in Costa Rica, millions of dollars in a vacant house wouldn't do us any good if it was seized. Once back on the freeway, I drove cautiously as I could while going over the different ways I could send the money to ourselves without it being traced to us.

I was planning to send three point five million dollars to Christina in

Barbados, and take onboard my flight three point five million dollars. I'd send the remainder to my mother.

With my heart beating faster with every green light I caught. I had to control myself as I grew more and more anxious. Upon meeting with my dad's friends Melvin just before the flight, he helped me separate the money into shoe boxes before putting them into large moving boxes, as he was going to ship the money to the addressees I wrote on the boxes.

With the monies that Donell had sent from St. Louis, I told Melvin to watch over it until he had heard from Donell or me telling him what to do with it next. After he agreed, I proceeded to meet with Wayne to get my passport.

"Man, shit got so crazy, I had to have you do me one last favor before I left."

"Well, anytime Don B. I guess I'm going to have to get a new connect now huh?" Wayne said playing his role to the *T* until the show was finally over..

Donell

Sitting on the hood of my Ferrai Enzo, I meditated on the new Mercedes Maybach 57s that I'd much rather have had. Since Id been kicking it with Danny D, I learned that he was more like my than I realized. Although I met him through Barry, we never really hit off. From the way he would just sit back and watch everything happen, to just always staying two steps ahead reminded me of my brother.

I had no idea how fast word would spread of me being in Memphis, everything seem like an epiphany. After all this time, I finally had the respect, the power and the right timing in my corner. It seemed as though every real hustler in the south, Midwest and other cities out east found me.

They all had heard of the Money Mobb Mafia and wanted to work for me. I was meeting more and more heavy hitters to the point where I bought Hosea out of everything he had stashed. With me at the head of the table now, I ran everything differently. Since it was only me and Danny, not to mention we still were on the Feds' radar, Danny and I scored the drugs, took the orders and delivered it all off our pagers. Deep in thought at how smoothly everything was running, we were distracted when we heard a car skid not far from my estate.

"Man Donnie, this is the life."

Looking past Danny, I was caught off guard to see a dump truck approaching being that the trash truck had just ran yesterday.

"Man what the fuck is that?"

Slightly leaning forward, I saw the truck stop two houses down from mine as the uniformed workers exited the back wearing all black.

"Where the hell all them cars going, Donnie?" Danny D said pointing at the opposite end of the street while reaching for his pistol at the same time. Witnessing the long line up of sedans, my heart skipped a beat as I jumped from off my hood.

BOOM . . . SHISHI . . . BOOM!

Watching Danny fly over the hood of my car was unreal as the shells from the shotgun lifted him up and over the car.

"Get out of the car! Get out of the car now! Mr. McCoy," The white man wearing the dump truck uniform said as he got on the ground in the kneeling position, aiming at me.

I closed my door and took one last look over my shoulder at Danny. The horrific swelling, the pool of blood pouring out from his chest was surreal.

"If you don't get outside the car McCoy, we have the authority to shoot you in it!"

BOOM . . . SHISHI . . . BOOM!

As they blew the air out of my car tires before surrounding me, they handcuffed and took me into custody while raiding my house in the process.

Barry

Headed to catch my private charter flight, it was all worth coming back to Dallas to make sure that Ronnie was okay and safe. I felt even more relieved to know that I would be able to see my son in a matter of hours. Mentally exhausted, I intended to sleep all the way until my plane landed.

At this point, just hearing that Donell was safe was good enough for me, but I wasn't going to miss another day of peace of mind. No more looking over my shoulder, talking in codes, and wearing bulletproof vests. Reclined in my seat, sipping Hennessy and Coke, I laid back at ease in the eight-person jet. With only two other people and myself, I had no worries. I closed my eyes as I waited for the flight to take off.

When I noticed the flight still hadn't taken off, I checked my watch and seen it was twenty minutes past one o'clock. *We were supposed to leave twenty minutes ago,* I thought to myself as I opened my eyes to see the cockpit door closed and the ladder ramp already let up. Avoiding eye contact with me, the stewardesses hurriedly turn the corner as I begin to ask her what the hell was going on.

"Just wait a little bit," I heard one of the white men whispering behind me.

"Hey, what's going on up there!"

Turning around to face the men that where whispering behind me, I heard voices coming from the cockpit.

"Get on the ground! Get on the ground now!"

Just when I felt my heart jump into my throat, one of the men behind jumped on top of me as I was a football fumble. From in front and behind, agents emerged from everywhere, as the ramp was now down. *I've been set the fuck up.*

It was as if they all knew I would be on here. I felt like I was dreaming the way they all swarmed the small plane and stood everywhere on the their phones and ear pieces.

"Well well well, if it isn't Don *B* 'The Godfather.' I told you we were going to catch up with you," Agent Logan said hovering over me with his hands inside his raincoat as the field agents stood me up to cuff my hands behind my back. It was then when I saw who had betrayed me walk onboard wearing a U.S. Marshall sweat jacket.

"Mr. Barry McCoy, I want you to meet undercover Detective Terry Wayne Johnson."

Chapter 33

Judgment Day

"Betrayal is the only truth that sticks."

—Arthur Miller

Detective Johnson

I KNEW THAT WHAT I was doing was right, but deep down inside I felt more nervous than ever. I had been undercover soo long and this was the moment that everyone was waiting for: the judge, U.S. Attorney, Grand Jury and most importantly, Barry and Donell.

The whole trial took longer than any DEA prosecutor had expected. Barry and Donell's criminal defense attorneys were cunning and manipulative. Everyday for the past five months, I had heard rumors of how the trial could go either way. My colleagues were constantly carrying on about how smart Barry had been, or at least acted in terms of concealing his dealings and actions compared to his younger brother Donell.

"That Jewish attorney Barry has is really giving the prosecutors a run for their money."

Upon Logan's request, I wore a black hoodie over my head as I was escorted through a back entrance into the courtroom for my own protection.

"Today we're going to put the nail in the coffin," Logan proudly boasted as he and Jim Reed escorted me to the courtroom. After all the verbal manipulation that Barry and Donell's attorneys were carrying on between the jurors and witnesses, there wasn't really anything concrete enough to link Barry directly to his accused position as the leader of the Money Mobb Mafia. Even after the testimonies of local politicians, extorted contractors, and the Mayor of San Antonio, his defense attorneys had evidence on all their under the table affairs that was more than damaging to their testimony, thanks to their Uncle Billy's meeting rooms.

After removing the hoodie from my head, Logan stood in front of me and stared me straight in my eyes.

"I don't know if you realize it or not but you're going to do more than you think. You're not only going to put this whole organization away for good, but you're our main agent who's knowledge is essential, making you a asset to this trial. Now is the time that you can prove to everyone else how bad you want this, and to really make an impact on the criminals that corrupt our neighborhoods. You understand me?"

I nodded as Logan finished his pep talk. Little did Logan know, even though this was the first case I would testify against someone in such a murderous organization, I was more than ready. Thinking back to Mike Millan and Detective Jacobs, I was more than ready to let the truth be known in full, along with all the details that came with it.

Barry

These mothafuckers just won't stop, I thought to myself holding a nonchalant attitude toward all the allegations and charges I was facing. After all these months on trial, I accepted the fact that I was going to be doing some serious time, but with having certain cases dismissed, there still was a possibility that I might be free once again on parole.

Even though my brother and I weren't being housed in the county jail anymore, the fact still remained that we were able to do whatever we wanted. From the Warden to just about the entire staff at the Dawson State Jail, I was treated with priority. I was eating pizza, wings, and fast food take out every other night. I even had the Sheriff acquire me a small flip phone until I was to be transferred. Nothing or no one was outside my reach. The only person not conveniently available to me was my son.

The Feds didn't have me on any wired phone conversations discussing anything illegal or contemplating any illegal acts, let alone violence. Though my attorney Robert Stewart was sly enough to create doubt about my orchestrated involvement in several homicide cases, there wasn't much my attorney could do to remove the doubt placed into the jurors' minds as far as my association with the alleged enforcers. The U.S Attorney General presented the grand jury with pictures of me and JD, Des and Jr shopping at the Lennox Mall in Atlanta and having lunch together at Houston's restaurant in Washington, D.C.

Maybe I'll do twenty-five if not thirty. Hell, tax evasion, racketeering and money laundering weren't anywhere as serious as a murder charge. But these God damn conspiracy charges ain't no joke. That shit is probably what will bring me down.

The most damaging confessions come from mid-level Mobb members who I had known since my sophomore year in college. I was taken back to see all the hustlers that were friends with Des, Junior and myself now turn into informants and codefendants. The same dudes clinging onto my shoulder at the New Years concert, were among those who lied on me if not agreed to everything the U.S. Attorney accused me of.

"They're actually going to let this mothafucka take the stand after all the dirt he's done?" I said under my breath when I laid eyes on Detective Wayne who stood near a door on the opposite side of the courtroom.

"Your Honor, we would now like to call Undercover D.E.A. Agent Terry Wayne Johnson to the stand."

As the Federal Prosecutors continued on with their presentation of pictures and seized guns from raids, they looked to Johnson to confirm my involvement as well as several other big Bosses I dealt with. Johnson testified against and dropped the dime on everybody, from Kingston to even people who were dead like Danny D and Stanley.

"Detective Johnson, can you explain to the Grand Jury what Barry McCoy's title was and what if not how his involvement affected the infamous Money Mobb Mafia?"

"Yes, I can," he said before clearing his throat. "Barry was without a doubt the head and leader of the Money Mobb Mafia organization. He was the person at the top of the chain. There was no one above him."

"Could you elaborate and clarify to the court as to the extent of those dealings?"

"Yes. Barry himself, if not his younger brother Donell, would issue paid-for murders on other drug dealers that didn't cooperate or abide by their rules. Donell frequently issued paid-for murders as well, that were in the interests of his close colleagues, such as Stanley Robinson. I personally witnessed Donell have a hand in a murder."

"Would you tell us the name and job title of this person Detective Johnson?"

"Yes, it was a fellow Agent of the Bureau, Detective Jacobs, whose job description was to pose as an undercover arms dealer until his cover was exposed by Detective Kyle Thomas."

"So not only are you saying that Barry McCoy headed the organization along with his brother, who posed as the second in charge, but he also dealt with corrupt law enforcement as well?"

"Yes, he did. I was used to make payments to crooked local police officers, Lieutenants and Captains who were on the Money Mobb Mafia payroll."

As the Federal Prosecutor went on to ask Detective Wayne to elaborate, and explain on what all he had witnessed and partook in, I knew that this was the one. Detective Wayne was the one informant who indeed was there when I gave the green light for Kyle's murder as well as a few others. Faced with new information provided by Johnson, I was limited in providing my attorney leeway as they tried to pierce Detective Johnson's character and intentions of being a reputable informant due to the Federal Corruption from within the Bureau.

Donell

I wish I could hang that mothafucka by his balls and set his ass on fire, I thought to myself, filled with anger as the U.S. Attorney used Johnson to answer and resolve practically all my pending cases that could have been acquitted, if not appealed.

I should have taken the gun from JD and blown that son of a bitch's head off myself that day in the barbershop, I thought trying my best to stay seated and calm in the courtroom.

"Detective Johnson, would you please clearly state your role and duties in the Money Mobb Mafia organization?

"I was a courier within the organization which included receiving and delivering money, drugs, and guns as well as being a reliable driver for kidnappings and home invasions. I also secured homes in their names."

"Would these homes be on the list of lavish estates that you see before you today?" The U.S. Attorney said as he held up a sheet of paper that was halfway full that he read aloud for the entire court room to hear.

"Mansions such as a home on Tuxedo Drive in Atlanta, GA; Ponte Vedra Beach and Bal Harbor, Florida; Holmby Hills in West Los Angeles; River Oaks in Houston; and two homes in Sugar Land, Texas."

"Yes, that is correct."

The U.S. Attorney then began showing the Grand Jury pictures of me driving cars I owned, from my Ferraris to the Lamborghinis. Although it was obvious as to what I did for a living, I still felt competent with who I had hired. William Murphy and Philip Banks were Federal Practitioners that had published books on legal studies based on their specialized experience and exceptional track record of acquitted cases.

"If you think you're losing leverage on the grounds of me getting an appeal, then ya'll better think of a way to counter that shit." I remembered telling my lawyers in a threatening tone this morning when they came to address my cases.

"Detective Johnson, in terms of Donell McCoy, on what accounts have you witnessed Donell issue a paid-for murder upon one of his competitors, if not a foe?" The U.S. Attorney asked while facing him. Before he interrupted Johnson himself only to walk away and rephrase his question. "I'm sorry for being so vague. I meant to ask you what part did Donell play in orchestrating a murder for hire upon those he felt were a threat to him? Men such as Stanley Robinson, Police Chief Atkins, and Darius "Slim" Johnson?"

"I've heard him speak of those people when he would refer to others who had 'to be dealt with.'" Detective Johnson responded as he leaned closer to the microphone, placing his final words in quotation marks with his hands.

"By saying 'dealt with,' you mean 'had to be killed,' correct?"

"Yes, that's correct."

The more this rat ass punk stayed on the stand, the more I became infuriated. My attorney never missed the opportunity to cross examine Johnson and ask him questions in terms of the legitimacy of his accusations, especially after I informed my lawyer of the murder Johnson committed in Nashville, Tennessee with Stanley. To my surprise, he covered his tracks very well. Obviously the DEA had already intimidated Stanley goons into saying otherwise on the stand. As if my shit wasn't already stinking up the whole courthouse, if there was ever one juror in any doubt, it was silenced when the Federal Prosecutor extracted a wiretapped conversation in the courtroom the next day.

"See, um..." The audio tape repeated out loud, echoing a recorded conversation between Detective Johnson and me that was as clear as could be. "Man, we weren't always doing it this big. We started off robbing bank trucks and trains, and from there we would get shipments of guns, retail items and other stuff. And then before you know it, we got into the drugs. At first we were just selling a hundred to two hundred bricks out in town and to other players in bigger cities. And then, once we dealt with Big John, we were moving like five hundred to eight hundred kilos and pounds a week to hustlers in damn near every other state."

"Yea, we're out here doing it big like Griselda Blanco," Stanley said in the background as the audio tape came to an end. As if this audio tape wasn't evidence enough as much as it was undeniable, the U.S. Attorney went on to ask one final question before allowing Detective Johnson to leave the stand.

"With that tape of Mr. McCoy and his deceased colleague in the background confirming their involvement in drugs, would you be able to elaborate on your carrier deliveries from the drug proceeds?"

"I would drive to Houston, Baton Rouge, Little Rock, and sometimes even to Arizona carrying shipments as large as one thousand kilos of cocaine and returning with as much as three to four million dollars in profit. This was all money from drugs transactions, not to mention hundreds of thousands of dollars from extortion that the Money Mobb Mafia was involved in."

As my attorneys went on to recall several witnesses who tried to revitalize my reputation as a business mogul, my thoughts began drifting off into my current standing in the local jail were I was being housed.

Due to Barry being as powerful as he was, and myself being the more influential and charismatic brother, the Warden decided that it would be better to transfer Barry and leave me in Decker Jail. It was then when I made up my mind that if I didn't stand a chance at being free again, I would just make the most of being incarcerated.

After the first two months of trial, I had already gotten together a crew from within the county jail that consisted of Money Mobb Mafia members who were awaiting trial and those awaiting sentencing. Barry didn't want to partake or be anywhere near my newfound plans, as he was afraid that he might lose his visiting rights with his son later on down the line.

I'm winning. Hell, they can't stop me. I been winning for so long, that even when the odds are against me, I can still win.

After the break before the verdict reading, I thought about how my brother's case had went and how he was charged with being the leader of the Mobb. But for ordering the murder of Detective Kyle, he still had to swallow a life sentence.

"Mr. Donell Stevens McCoy, you have been lawfully tried in this court and found guilty to all charges brought forward against you including engaging in a criminal enterprise, two counts of money laundering, two counts of fencing, conspiracy to violate narcotic laws, one count of interstate travel in aid of racketeering and eight counts of using a public telephone for illegal purposes and three counts of premeditated murder."

"Since you have declined speaking any final words, the Federal court releases you into the custody of the Attorney General of the United States and hereby sentences you to two consecutive life sentences without the possibility of parole."

Profanity filled the courtroom, as some people were upset due to the fact that I didn't get placed on death row. On the other hand, some people in the court were upset that Detective Johnson participated in the organization's activities, not to mention knew of corruption within the Bureau and continued to pursue their investigation as if nothing happened.

Chapter 34

The Aftermath

"... See to live is to suffer but to survive, Well that's to find meaning in the suffering..."   *DMX—Slippin*

SIX MONTHS LATER....

"*I KNOW YOU don't smoke weed. I know this. But I'm going to get you high today 'cause its Friday, you ain't got no job and you ain't got shit to do.*"

Man... I'm sick of this shit, I thought to myself.

"*When you do good things, good things comeback to you. And when you do bad things, you can expect unfortunate results...*" If I had to hear the lady in our physical therapy class repeat that saying one more time, I was going to strangle her with those same annoying loud ass colorful beads she wore faithfully. Since I had been in ICU, I ended up having two blood transfusions before they released me a month ago. For about five weeks now, I've been attending physical therapy to learn all the things I once took for granted. I had to learn how to walk, breathe, and exercise all over again.

Mrs. Jenkins was an exceptional nurse through out my whole recovery. She often tried to cheer me up when I would reminisce on all the bad luck I had. I often thought about how JD was setup, and how both my parents were dead. Sometimes I just wondered why I had to be the one that made it. I mean, as far as I could remember up until when I got here, I was the one that did the most wrong.

Since I had gotten shot in the parking lot, all I could remember was the young kid who shot me and opening my eyes only to see Barry by my side. I remembered squeezing his hand to express my thanks since I didn't have the strength to do so verbally. Every time I had turned on the television when I wasn't watching a movie, I was hearing about the ongoing trial of my brothers:

"*The Money Mobb Mafia's—better known to their rivals and adversaries as the Murder Money Mafia—operations have been dismantled by the United States Government. Alleged and accused leader, Mobb Boss Barry Brad McCoy along with one hundred and seventy-five other co-conspirators are being charged with Continuing a Criminal Enterprise or aiding the illegal Criminal activist in promoting their mayhem . . .*

"*. . . . Now with CBS news exclusive, the U.S. government has indicted and arrested most of the top tier of the largest drug trafficking and money laundering network recorded in history. Let me remind you that the Money Mobb Mafia drug smuggling scheme exceeded profits at a net worth of twenty million dollars every month. This amount, reported from several informants from within the organization, is only the tip of the iceberg, since the Money Mobb Mafia extorted dozens of business owners.*

Today's final sentencing ending with tables being turned over as the underboss of the Money Mobb Mafia, Donell McCoy, threw a chair at the judge after receiving his sentencing. The once statewide leading scorer, McDonald High School MVP, was apprehended in Memphis outside his illustrious mansion with over two point seven million dollars and a 2001 Ferrari Enzo in his possession. Federal Drug Enforcement Agency confiscated over two hundred kilos of cocaine, heroin, marijuana and about a dozen gallons of prescribed promethazine.

I couldn't believe how the Feds had everything already figured out. Everything we thought they didn't know, they knew. I mean *everything*. It was all over the news and still taking place downtown. I didn't know where I stood in the middle of all the rumors I was hearing.

"Good morning Mr. McCoy." Nurse Jenkins said smiling. "I see you're still looking at the news huh? Baby you can't trouble yourself with the affairs of your cousins. They brought all those consequences upon themselves. Them boys' mother got to be just heartbroken. She comes in here three times a week on her way home from court to check on you."

"I know right."

"Whenever I talk to their mother Juanita, my heart goes out to her. I see how come Barry wanted you to be under confidential disclose. There's still one of the main members at large and by the way the police describe him, he is indeed a threat to society. Calvin Marshall is a bad man. He's murdered so many people. They said the District Attorney has several cases that are considered Capital Punishment that he is responsible for."

"Oh yeah?"

"The police don't even have a consistent picture of him because of all the wigs, and shades he wore. It's as if he doesn't exist. By the way, here's the number Barry gave me. I believe it's to a cab driver."

"I remember when he gave me that in the ambulance truck. It was as if he knew the police were coming for him. It must be kind of creepy knowing that your days as a free man are coming to end."

"Make me feel kind of eerie if you ask me," she said as she exited the room. I unfolded the napkin. It read: *Ole School—214 918 4799.*

Barry

Laying in my bottom bunk, all I ever did now was look out my cell to the tier behind the open bars. I felt empty. My mind was completely blank and my heart was filled with remorse. The circus was finally over and my days as a free man were long behind me with nothing but memories to keep my mind company.

My mother came to my trial at the end during sentencing because I didn't want her to actually hear and witness all the evidence, not to mention the recorded conversations presented against me. I would rather her heard the news and not know what to believe instead of seeing of all the wrongdoing I was involved in. Sitting up, I couldn't help but dwell on all the times I could have done things differently. And some things I wish I hadn't done at all.

Walking down the tier, my reputation overshadowed everyone. But unlike my brother, there weren't any good feelings that resulted from everything I made happen in the game. The bottom line was that I was leaving my only son behind in exchange for this so called reputation.

When I dialed the country code to Costa Rica, I felt as though I had no business calling Brandi after letting her down twice with broken promises and a son without a father. Standing in the conjugal visiting room, I used my cell phone to make contact with everyone I wanted to talk to nowadays.

"Hello?"

"Hello."

"Oh, hey," Brandi responded realizing it was me before she continued. "It's okay Barry. I'm a big girl, I'm going to be alright. You know, at first I was really broken up," she said trying to refrain from breaking down into tears. "But I still love you. I always will love you. You always will have a special place in my heart because I see you everyday," she said sniffling. "I get to wake up to your face everyday and that much I'm grateful for . . . Even if I can't have the man I want to share my life with." Busting into tears, she whimpered as she tried to finish her sentence. "I got all the money, all the furniture and all of everything. I tried to give your mom some of it, but she said I should keep it."

As I fought to find the best words of closure that would comfort her, I found myself tongue-tied, just as I was when I walked out on her when she stood crying at the airport. I wanted to tell that her I got all the letters, pictures of her, Junior and of us in college, but that would have not made things any better.

"Well. Tell my little man I love him. I guess we can stay in touch." I said before my phone lost signal.

Ronnie

After the hospital midnight shift begun, the nurses who just started working made their rounds checking on the patients. Little did they know that I was one patient they wouldn't have to account for after tonight. Aunt Juanita smiled after I told her where I was going and who'd be meeting me there. Overjoyed, she hugged me and volunteered to buy me some clothes to go see Christina in.

If the police hadn't put two and two together that I was Calvin Marshall then they might as well blew their chance, I thought while packing my duffle bag with hygiene items and my passport paperwork. Kneeling down, I ducked under the nurses' desk before bear-crawling out of my section of the hospital and into the elevator. Once inside the elevator, I changed from my hospital gown into the clothes inside my duffle bag. Speedwalking out the lobby, I spotted Ole School's yellow cab not far before I opened the door and eased into the back seat.

"Fam, how you living?" He said, lowering his paper from his face as if he was already expecting me.

"I'm living, and that's good enough for me." I said leaning back and placing my hoody over my head. Checking his side mirrors, he slowly pulled away from the hospital.

"Yo fam, I remember when I last seen you."

"I'm glad you pulled through yo. I sure hate Barry couldn't make it out. He was so damn close, too."

"Oh yeah?"

"Hell yeah, fam. He was on the news when they caught him on that private plane…On his way to Costa Rica that same night. They said he had some three point five million dollars in cash with him."

"Oh yeah."

"Yeah yeah. He thought the plane was going take off, but it never did. It was a setup. That was the same day that he flew in to see you," He said, looking back at me through the rearview mirror.

It all made since now, Barry had literally traded his life for mine. Had he not came back for me, he'd been a free man. Merging onto I-35, I couldn't do nothing but sit back and be grateful for being free.

As the night came and went, so did I. I had an eight hour plane ride where I caught flights from Dallas to Atlanta before finally landing at the Grantley Adams International Airport in Barbados. Like B.I.G said, "It was all a dream" the way everything looked and was now. From the see-through water to the sandy white beaches, palm trees covered the beach houses and people playing water sports all across the coastline. When the plane finally landed, I blended in like a chamelleon with all the tourists and people who had family members awaiting their arrival.

"Good afternoon sir. Where to?" The cab driver asked as I motioned for him to drive from the airport immediately.

"You just drive and I'll tell you when to make turns, okay?" I said with my attention focused outside the back window checking for tails. "Alright… A litter further up ahead…. Turn on the next block and stop at the last house."

"You have some very wealthy friends," the driver said nervously trying to ease the tension in the cab.

"Yeah man, here's a tip too," I said, handing him twice as much as the ride actually cost.

Cautiously stepping out of the cab, I scanned the perimeter, suspecting anything. Still not convinced that I was off *scot free*, I exited and headed toward some bushes in the driveway next to my SUV where I retrieved a pistol and tucked it into my pants.

HONK HONK!

The cab sounded as it drove off. From the timed water sprinklers to the little kids walking by my new neighbors' houses, I couldn't believe it. After everything I'd been through, I was actually free. Even though I had a house key, I still rung the doorbell looking through the translucent windows and over my shoulder at the same time. All I saw was tourists walking by with cameras on their way to the beach without a care in the world.

"Who is it?"

"It's me baby," I said as she pulled back the massive door only to be standing there with some Frederick's lingerie on. Shaking my head with a grin on my face, I knew I didn't have to have my guard up any longer. Closing the door behind me, the moment her eyes met mines felt as if I was seeing her for the first time. Christina's eyes said it all.

"Don't ever scare me like that again Ron." She said leading me into our living room. Passing by moving boxes on the floor, I was reminded of Barry and Donell one more time when I seen the pictures of us Christina had decorated the house with.

"Barry sent that box for you before he got caught up... That one right there."

Moving toward it, I noticed a note that was caught up in the duct tape still hanging onto the box. Never being unfolded until now, the yellow paper stood out in the midst of all the big face dollar bills bulging through the box.

I love ya... I'll see you on the other side.

-Barry